"This book is a mystery masterpiece. It has a great build-up and a shocking ending. *Anna Smudge: Professional Shrink* puts you in the middle of all of the action. I loved it so much, I was heartbroken when it ended."
    —Allen Alvarado (Discovery Kids' *Flight 29 Down*)

"The world is a safer place with Anna Smudge in it! Clever twists, hints that keep you guessing and a good dose of action, this book is an easy recommendation for readers who enjoy memorable characters and stories. Here's hoping for a television version of this exciting series!"
    —Denise Bradley, editor-in-chief, *KEWL Magazine*

"One of the best mysteries I have ever read.... The author, MAC, achieved a feeling of suspense, mystery, and humor throughout the whole book."
    —*Flamingnet*

"What fun! A mystery novel designed for kids with a gutsy and intelligent heroine who never talks down to her prime audience."
    —Karyn Bowman, managing editor,
    Family Time Magazine

"After I was done reading it I was left wondering two very important things: How long before I get my hands on the sequel and just what do I do now with the hyperactive seven year old in my home who thinks she's Anna Smudge?"
    —Joe Quesada, editor-in-chief, *Marvel Comics*

THE PROFESSIONALS

BOOK 1

ANNA SMUDGE
Professional Shrink

BY **MAC**

ILLUSTRATIONS BY *GLENN FABRY*

Toasted Coconut Media · New York

For my loving parents,
Paul & Franci

You taught me to look both ways before crossing the street.

And reminded me that there are always good things
waiting on the other side.

ANNA SMUDGE: PROFESSIONAL SHRINK. Copyright © 2008 by Melissa A. Calderone. All rights reserved. Published by Toasted Coconut Media. No part of this book may be used, reproduced, or transmitted in any form by any means, electronic or mechanical, including photocopying, recording, or any information storage and retrieval system, without written permission, except in the case of brief quotations embodied in critical articles or reviews. For information regarding permissions, contact Toasted Coconut Media, 200 Second Avenue, 4th floor, Suite 40, New York, NY, 10003.

www.ToastedCoconutMedia.com
www.WhoIsMrWho.com

Design by Gregory P. Collins

Library of Congress Control Number: 2007909656

Publisher's Cataloging-in-Publication Data

MAC, 1977–
    Anna Smudge : professional shrink / by MAC ; illustrations by Glenn Fabry.
        p. cm.
    Series: The Professionals, book 1.
    ISBN 978-1-934906-00-2
    Summary: While giving therapy to every nut in Manhattan, sixth grade shrink, Anna Smudge, must catch the criminal mastermind, Mr. Who, and save her father.
    1. Mystery and detective stories. 2. Psychologists—Juvenile fiction.
3. New York (City)—Juvenile fiction. 4. Fathers and daughters—Juvenile fiction. I. Fabry, Glenn. II. Title. III. Series.

PZ7.M11184 An 2008
[Fic]—dc22
                                                                        2007909656

First U.S. Paperback Edition: May 2008
Printed in Canada.

10 9 8 7 6 5 4 3 2 1

CONTENTS

ANNA SMUDGE
Professional Shrink

Prologue

Anna Smudge sat in jail.

Well, not exactly jail. She sat on a tall bench in the waiting room of Police Precinct 19, her legs dangling off the edge. Nine days ago, if anyone had told Anna that she'd end up here, she would've said they were nuts. Then again, nine days ago her life had been completely different...nine days ago she had been a nobody...nine days ago she had been Smudge, "the Sludge."

"Lemme go, cop dude! Lemme go!" A police officer pushed a tall skinny man in handcuffs through the door. "I'm gonna change! No more stealing, I promise! I'm gonna be a new man! I'm gonna live on the straight and narrow, for real!"

The skinny man skidded to a halt when he saw Anna. *"It's you,"* he breathed. The officer tried to push him on, but the skinny man wouldn't budge. He stared at Anna, his large bug eyes nearly popping from his long, thin face. "You're that girl, aren't you? You're her! That's you, isn't it?"

Anna nodded.

"Can you help me? Please! I don't wanna be a criminal anymore!"

Anna slid off the bench and placed one of her business cards in his cuffed hand. "When you get out, give me a call."

The police officer stared at Anna strangely as he led a much quieter man toward the jail cells in back.

"Anna Smudge." A stern officer behind the desk eyed her curiously. "The Chief will see you now."

Anna nodded and reached for her backpack.

"Hey, you're that girl, aren't you?"

Anna smiled mysteriously and entered the gated area.

The Chief's office was plastered with ripped-out newspaper articles; they covered the room like an odd sort of wallpaper. Anna let her eyes skim across the various headlines:

WHO IS THE MYSTERIOUS NEW CRIME BOSS?

MR. WHO STRIKES TERROR IN HEARTS OF NEW YORKERS!

MR. WHO SETS HITMAN DONNY
"THE MEATBALL" FRATELLI LOOSE!

"Miss Smudge, please have a seat," said a low, gritty voice.

"Thank you."

"My sister's a big fan."

The Chief of Police looked like a giant bulldog. He reached for a large mug and took a sip. "PTTTTEW!!

PTTAH!" He spit the liquid into his garbage, growling angrily. "Tastes like the Band Aid on my big toe! And it's cold!"

He picked up the phone. "Lieutenant, important police business. Get me a *hot* coffee!" He looked at Anna. "Want anything?"

Anna shook her head.

"And some donuts for Miss Smudge." The Chief slammed down the receiver and examined Anna with tired eyes. "Bad habit, coffee. I started when I was about your age. How old are you?"

"Eleven."

"Yup. Nasty habit, coffee. At least wait until junior high when they start piling on the paperwork." The Chief sighed. He looked like he hadn't slept in a week. "If what you're claiming is true, Miss Smudge, it could finally put an end to this racket." He motioned to the articles. "City's in an uproar! It's like Romper Room in the streets! I've put some of my best men on it, and they've come back chewed up and spit out!" The Chief clenched his large jaw. "So tell me, Miss Smudge, who is *he?*"

Anna opened her mouth to reply when—

CLANK! CLANK! CLANK! CLANK!

"What on earth's that noise?" yelled the Chief.

A lieutenant stuck his head through the door. He glanced at Anna before turning to the Chief. "Sir, it's the inmates. They know she's here. They...they want a group session, sir."

"Well, quiet them down."

"How, sir?"

"I don't know. Sing 'em a lullaby!" The Chief waved the lieutenant from the room. Exhausted, he leaned back in his chair. When he finally spoke, his voice was a hoarse whisper.

"You know, the FBI told me he didn't exist. The CIA said he was just a myth. On the streets they call him the Boogeyman. But all along, I knew in my gut he was real!" The Chief turned to Anna, his eyes gleaming. "Who is he, Miss Smudge? Who is Mr. Who?"

Anna opened her mouth.

"Wait! Start at the very beginning. Tell me everything!"

"Everything?"

"Yeah, everything."

Anna closed her eyes and listened to the clanking...and began to remember how it all started.

9 Days Ago

CLANK, CLANK, CLANK...The guard's boots clanked against the metal floor of the prison like a sledgehammer...CLANK, CLANK...He was just finishing his rounds, checking all the prison cells along the long hallway. He was about to turn around to head back to his desk when he heard a voice.

"Help! Somebody!"

The guard looked tentatively toward a door that led to the High-Security Ward, where they kept the most dangerous prisoners.

"Is somebody there? Help!"

The guard took his heavy key ring from his belt and unlocked the door. In this wing of the prison, the jails had no bars. The prisoners were kept in individual cells surrounded by four unbreakable walls and no windows. The voice was louder now.

"HEY! CAN SOMEBODY HELP!"

The guard approached the cell where the voice was coming from. The name on the door read *Donny "the Meatball" Fratelli.* The guard had heard this name before. This prisoner had once been the most famous hitman in New York.

"YO! I CAN HEAR YOUR FOOTSTEPS! CAN YOU HELP ME OUT?"

The guard nervously cleared his throat. "Um, what's wrong?"

There was a sigh of relief. "Thanks for answering, boss. I've been callin' out forever. I need some help." There was an embarrassed laugh. "Ya see, I kinda got myself in a little situation here…"

"What's wrong?" the guard said, trying to peer through a narrow slot in the door.

There was another embarrassed laugh. "Well, I'm stuck on the can."

"The can?" the guard repeated.

"Yeah. You know, the can, the pot, the porcelain throne… the toilet…the place where smart folks write really good poetry. I'm stuck here. I ran out of toilet paper."

"Well, I'm not really supposed to be in this ward—"

"Come on, buddy, I've been stuck here for over an hour! Have a heart! My butt's all numb."

The guard hesitated for a moment. Then he turned to see a storage closet behind him. He opened the door and shined his flashlight inside, spotting a large box of Charmin. "OK," he called. "I've got a roll for you. Just, um, stay where you are. I'll toss the roll inside.

"Yeah, sure thing, boss!" the voice said, gratefully. "Thanks a load!" Then there was a laugh. "Get it? Load? Thanks a load—and I'm in the bathroom!"

The guard held his nose with one hand and fumbled for his keys with the other. This had certainly not been in the job description, he thought, sticking the roll of toilet paper through a small crack in the door as quickly as possible. Unfortunately, it was not quick enough. A humongous hand grabbed the guard's wrist and yanked him effortlessly through the door.

"What the—NO! NO! NOT THE PLUNGER!"

All that could be heard was the guard's screams, muffled by the soft squish of the toilet-bowl plunger. Then there was a flush.

.●.

The very large man put on the guard's much smaller clothes. They didn't look that great on him, but he wasn't too worried about making a fashion statement. It was time to bust out of this joint. There was someplace he *had* to be.

Thinking it would make a very smart disguise, the large man stuck the stringy white top of a mop on his head. He rolled a mop and pail out from the storage closet, and like a very large janitor with really bad hair, he slowly wheeled his way through the prison hallways and toward the front door.

"Hey, you!"

The large man began to walk faster.

"You! I haven't seen you before. Got an ID card?"

The large man began to run.

"HEY, STOP THAT MAN!"

He hopped on the back of the large plastic pail he was wheeling and pushed off as hard as he could.

"CATCH THAT MAN!"

A number of guards lunged toward him, but like a very large bowling ball, he plowed right through them. The front door was coming up ahead. An astonished guard jumped to his feet. The large man lifted the mop from the pail he was riding on, and with one fell swoop, the guard was down.

An alarm began to sound. Footsteps...lots of them... pounded on the sidewalk behind him. The large man used the mop in his hand to push off on the ground again...and then again...trying to roll faster...and just when the group of guards was catching up, just when they were about to tackle the very large man, cuff him, and drag him back to his high-security cell...a car whizzed around the corner. The large man turned, grinning evilly at the guards. Then he squatted down and grabbed hold of the car's bumper as it speeded by.

CHAPTER 1

Wishful Thinking

"You're dead, Smudge!"

The words hung in the chilly air like a mist.

Anna shivered and rubbed her hands together to warm them. Her class was on the school roof, which was enclosed on all sides by a towering chain link fence. They were playing dodgeball.

Jacob Pierce crouched behind the white line of the opposing team, his freckled face drawn into a wicked snarl. "You ready to die, Smudge?" He pounded a dodgeball with one hand. "D-E-A-D," he spelled out slowly.

A whistle sounded and Jacob hurled the ball at Anna with a loud war cry. Anna watched as the ball whizzed toward her...speeding faster...and faster...and then, at the very last minute, she jumped high into the air and did a perfect split over the ball. Shocked, Anna landed back on the tarmac with a soft thud. She had no idea she could do that! Apparently, her classmates didn't either, because they began to talk in frantic whispers to one another.

"Smudge has the ball!" Ms. McGee called.

Anna clasped the dodgeball in shaky hands, took a deep breath, and stepped up to the white line.

"Don't do it, Smudge," Jacob growled. "I'll make you regret it for the rest of your slow, pathetic, little life."

"*Slow?*" Anna said with a smile, and when the whistle blew she hurled the ball at Jacob with a speed she didn't know she had. The ball shot forward like a bolt of lightning, faster than anything anyone had ever seen. It smacked Jacob in the chest, sending him flying across the rooftop in a red blur until he bashed into the chain link fence and collapsed onto the tarmac with a loud clump.

Cheers erupted and everyone roared, "Anna! Anna! Anna!"

Anna looked around her and realized that it wasn't just her team that was cheering; both teams were yelling her name and running toward her. She turned, and Todd Brecken-Bayer was beside her, his blue eyes twinkling. "Anna, you're amazing!"

And then her parents pushed through the crowd, their faces beaming. "We're so proud, pumpkin!" cried Anna's father. "We love you!" He lifted her high into the air as all of her schoolmates crowded around, patting her on the back, chanting,

"Anna! Anna! Anna!...Anna...Anna, Anna, you're late. Wake up, Anna."

.◦.

"Wake up, Anna! BZZZT! You'll be late for school! BZZZT!"

Anna opened her eyes to hear the hallway intercom crackling with a funny Irish voice. "Time to rise and face the mornin'!"

Anna slowly swung both legs over the side of her bed and padded through the Smudges' huge hallway, lined with expensive art from all over the world.

"BZZZT! Are you awake, Miss Anna?"

Anna reached for the intercom and pressed a button. "I'm up, Percy. Thanks," she told the downstairs doorman. She leaned against the wall, rubbing her eyes with the back of her hands. "Percy, I was having the greatest dream. I was—"

"Sorry to interrupt, Miss Anna," crackled Percy's voice. "But it's a wee bit busy in the lobby this morning. I've got a lot of cabs to hail. So no dilly-dallying."

Flicking on the light in her bathroom, Anna groaned when she saw her reflection. Her bangs were sticking straight up. She looked like a rooster. Well, no time for a shower this morning. Anna turned the water on and tried to flatten her hair with her fingertips, but it just seemed to have a mind of its own. After a few minutes, she gave up and moved on to her teeth, making sure to brush each tooth sufficiently, concentrating on the hard-to-reach places in the—"

"BZZT!" Percy's voice crackled through the intercom once again. "Miss Anna! What in the world are you doin' up there? You need to move along now. You're slower than molasses!"

Anna sighed and looked at herself one last time in the

mirror. *I will try to be faster,* she said to the messy-headed girl staring back at her. Then she turned toward her wardrobe and, as usual, made an attempt to pick up the pace.

A little while later, she was standing on the sidewalk next to a spiffy-looking Percy, who was dressed in a crisp blue and yellow uniform.

"Did Mother and Father have another early business meeting?" Anna asked him.

"Yes. They left at the crack of dawn."

Anna stared down at her sneakers disappointedly. "I bet they'll have a *late* meeting too, huh?

But Percy was too busy flagging a cab to answer.

"Have a great day at school, Anna!" Percy said, giving her a little pat and shutting the cab door.

As the cab zoomed down Park Avenue, Anna turned around in her seat and watched as her building became just another luxury high-rise that lined the streets of New York City. It was rush hour, Anna's least favorite time of the day. She pressed her forehead to the cool glass window and watched as streams of hurried people poured in and out of buildings. She eyed a well-dressed couple talking rapidly on their cell phones as they clicked down the street together, briefcases in hand. Anna thought of her parents. She wondered what they were doing right now…

The cab was almost at the Bendox School, turning down a traffic-packed Lexington Avenue, when it suddenly veered to a halt, causing Anna to reach her hands out to keep from being catapulted into the front seat.

"What in the world—" the cab driver yelled angrily. But just as the words left his mouth, he was silenced by the strangest sight. A large man with a large mop covering his face was riding a plastic pail on wheels, swinging from one car bumper to another like a crazy ape. Anna watched, mouth hanging open, as he zoomed past her cab. There was a loud BANG as he used a mop to push off against the cab door.

"Jeez! Watch the paint job!" yelled the driver.

Following the man on a pail, in steady pursuit, was a cascade of police cars, attempting to weave their way through the morning traffic, sirens blaring.

Anna turned around in her seat, her eyes wide, and watched the man on the pail zigzag down the block and disappear around the corner. Usually sirens and honking were old-hat in New York City, sometimes even a car chase, but a mop-and-pail chase?

"It's because it's Monday," the cab driver declared as he leaned on his horn. "All the nut jobs come out on Monday."

When the cab finally pulled up in front of the Bendox School, Anna sat there for a moment, staring at the large red doors, wishing she didn't have to go inside.

"Go on, kid. Get a move on. You're gonna be late!"

Anna turned to the driver, a pleading expression on her face. "Can't I just wait here until second period?"

He looked at Anna, bewildered. "Why would you wanna do that?"

"Because gym is first today."

"And what's so bad about gym?"

CHAPTER 2

Smudge "The Sludge"

"SLUDGE! SLUDGE! SLUDGE! SLUDGE!"

Anna stood smack in the middle of the dodgeball court, wishing she could sink into the ground and disappear. Jacob Pierce had gotten his entire team to chant the stupid nickname he had given her.

"SLUDGE! SLUDGE! SLUDGE!"

Jacob squatted and hurled the ball full speed at her.

Anna just stood there, frozen. For some reason, her legs were rooted to the ground like tree trunks. With an all too familiar feeling she watched as the rubber ball raced toward her, whizzing closer...and closer...and then—

Someone pushed her. Anna splayed onto the cold tarmac as the ball hit the gated fence behind her. When she looked up, she was mortified to see Todd Brecken-Bayer, a look of concern in his gorgeous blue eyes.

"Anna, you OK? Sorry to push you, but you weren't moving, and the ball was coming right at you and—"

"Smudge!" Ms. McGee's voice called out, "You O.K?"

"Yeah," Anna said, taking Todd's hand as he helped her up but nervously yanking it away when she realized he was actually touching her. "Yeah," she mumbled.

The bell rang, and everyone started toward the door.

"Next time, Sludge!" Jacob pushed by her with his cousin Roselyn. "I'm gonna get you. It'll be easy. You're so slow, it's like tagging a slug. And it's gonna hurt!" He slammed the door behind him and held it shut for a few minutes so Anna couldn't get out.

.●.

"Ugh, what a way to start out the week!"

Quenton Cohen strode down the hallway next to Anna, shaking his head in disgust. "That was out-of-control awful!"

Anna shrugged, not really wanting to talk about it.

"Seriously, that was worse than *Sock-iller!*"

"*Sock-iller?*" Anna repeated.

"Yeah, this really bad horror movie on cable about this smelly sock that comes to life and kills a whole soccer team. Really bad. I think it got zero stars or something."

"Why do you waste your time watching that stuff?"

Quenton shrugged. "What? I like to watch bad TV while I cook. And some things are so bad that they're funny." He raised his eyebrows. "But *that* was not funny-bad, that was just bad-bad."

Anna sighed, wishing Quenton would drop the subject. Jacob Pierce had made it his mission to make her life as miserable as possible. It was just another fact of life. Kind of like the fact that Anna was a slowpoke, a dawdler...a sludge.

"Listen, Anna," Quenton raised his hands in the air defensively. "I'm just saying that the caveman's getting worse. Jacob never used to be this bad. That was horrible!"

"Mondays are always horrible," Rachel Riley chimed in. "You have two whole days called the weekend to sleep late and do whatever you want, and then comes Monday, ruining everything!"

"Yeah, well, Monday's not the problem, Rach," Quenton interrupted. "The problem is Pierce. It's time to take a stand." He kicked open the door to the boy's locker room. "Conquer the Caveman!" he called as he disappeared inside.

"I agree with Quenton," said Rachel. "You know, my mom says that women should band together to create a society of strong women who..."

As they entered the girl's locker room, Rachel continued to chatter a mile a minute. But Anna enjoyed listening to her. That was one of the only things she felt she was good at—listening. But what good did that do anyone? It sure didn't fit in with the hustle and bustle of the Big Apple, and it sure wasn't like being good at gym or art or science or...

"Math!" cried Rachel, slamming her locker door. "Let's jet before Ms. Musashi blows a fuse."

Anna looked down; she was still wearing her gym clothes. "Um, I'm not really ready."

"Anna, what on earth have you been doing?"

"I was just thinking about—"

"Well, you better hurry up," Rachel warned. "If you're late again, Ms. Musashi will freak. And then she might use her stick on you. Is that thing even legal? I mean why does Ms. Musashi even carry a stick? It kind of looks like one of those whips that horse-back riders carry."

Rachel's face brightened. "I love horses! My mom says we can't possibly have a horse. It's not affordable. Plus, where would we keep it? In the bathtub? It's not practical having a horse in New York City. They don't have garages for them and—"

"I have a horse," Roselyn Pierce interrupted. She was standing by Rachel's locker, a cold smile playing at the corners of her kewpie-doll lips. She twirled a shiny lock of auburn hair around her finger. "I said, I have a horse."

Rachel looked at Roselyn with wide eyes, for once having nothing to say.

"I wanted a horse when I was a little girl, so my daddy bought a summer house in the Hamptons, with a barn in the back. Right, Amy?"

A shy girl standing behind Roselyn, like a tall slim shadow, peeked her head out and nodded.

"You know," Roselyn said, looking directly at Rachel, "my mom says that when you really love someone, you give them anything they want. I wanted a horse and my mother and father love me so much they gave me one. But you don't *have* a father, do you?"

Anna glared daggers at Roselyn. She was just as obnoxious as her cousin Jacob.

"Maybe your mom doesn't love you like you think,"

Roselyn continued in a syrupy voice. Amy Lerner stood quietly behind Roselyn looking extremely uncomfortable.

Rachel's bottom lip began to quiver. Suddenly the bell rang.

"The bell!" Roselyn quickly flounced out of the room with Amy in tow, leaving a silent Rachel in her wake.

Anna watched Rachel as she wiped her eyes on a dirty gym shirt, gathered up her stuff, and trudged from the locker room. She wished she could do something or say something to make her friend feel better. But instead she just leaned her head against a cold locker feeling helpless.

Anna stood outside the closed door of the math room, late. She took a deep breath and slipped inside, creeping toward her usual seat in the back row next to Quenton. When Quenton saw Anna he opened his eyes wide and mouthed, "Careful!"

Anna nodded, willing herself to be invisible. She was almost there, the empty desk just a few feet away. Quenton was frantically mouthing something, but Anna was so busy trying not to make a sound, and then it happened: Jacob stuck his leg out.

Anna tripped, falling onto a chair, which slammed into a desk, which in turn tumbled over onto the floor, making a little less noise than a train wreck. When Anna looked up, she saw Quenton groaning with his face in his hands, she heard Roselyn Pierce's laughter like the Wicked Witch of the West, and then...

CRACK! Anna jumped as Ms. Musashi's stick hit the chalkboard. "So nice of you to join us, Smudge," said a thin voice. "If you're not too busy disrupting class, maybe you can help us solve this decimal-division problem. The problem we are all supposed to be working on."

Sliding into her desk, Anna looked up at the board and tried to divide 16.9 by 6.5 in her head.

Just be fast. Just be fast.

A long moment passed, all eyes were on her...

"Smudge!" Ms. Musashi's voice called out impatiently, smacking her stick against her open palm. "Are we there yet?"

Anna was about to answer when Jacob lifted a straw and sent a spitball bulleting through the air. It landed right on target in Anna's mouth. Her voice stuck in the back of her throat as she gagged on the soggy piece of notebook paper.

"I—*kaAK!*"

"What's the matter, Smudge? Sludge on your tongue?" Jacob whispered. Roselyn giggled softly.

"Smudge!"

"*...ack...*"

As Anna hacked up the chewy projectile, all she could see was red—Jacob's red hair, his red T-shirt, his red freckles— as he grinned at her from his seat, revealing an ugly red tongue. She was so sick and tired of him doing this to her! So sick of the Pierces! Every day it was the same thing! And in front of Todd Brecken-Bayer this morning, how embarrassing!

"What's the matter, Sludge? You smudge in your pants?"

"Shut up, Jacob!" hissed Rachel.

"What are you going to do, Retarded Rachel?" Jacob whispered. "Go tell your welfare mom? Where's your dad? Where did he g—"

Suddenly, Anna reached out and grabbed a chunk of bright red hair, yanking it as hard as she could. She could hear Jacob yelling but still, she wouldn't let go. They fell onto the floor and rolled around, kicking desks out of the way.

CRACK! A long stick hit the floor between them, and a spindly arm reached out and in one swift motion pulled Jacob and Anna to their feet. Jacob let out a low, deep growl. Anna thought he might pounce on her, but when he looked up and saw Ms. Musashi, he glanced at Anna for a split second, grinned, and then started to wail.

"Don't let her hurt me, Ms. Musashi. Oh please, don't let her get me! Help!" Jacob dodged behind their math teacher as if frightened for his life.

Ms. Musashi glared at Anna. "Jacob, are you injured? Do you need to visit the infirmary?"

Jacob made his lower lip quiver like he was about to cry. "I'm just so scared. I turned around to see if she needed any help with that problem, and she attacked me. I was just trying to be nice! She bit me! Ahhh!"

"I did not bite him. He's lying!" Anna blurted out in disbelief.

"Miss Smudge!" Ms. Musashi said in a cold voice. "I am sending you to the principal's office."

Anna opened her mouth to protest but closed it as Jacob peeked his head out from behind Ms. Musashi, a sly grin on his face. He looked like the Cheshire cat.

"I do not permit this type of behavior in my class!" Ms. Musashi crossed to her desk and began to furiously scribble a note. She folded it neatly, sealed it, and handed it to Anna. "Take this with you to Principal Rollins's office. I'll be down later to talk with him myself."

Anna walked toward the door. She saw Quenton and Rachel watching with worried looks on their faces. And then she saw Todd Brecken-Bayer and felt her face flush bright red.

"Smudge," Ms. Musashi called out in a voice that could cut steel. "I have my eye on you."

The very large man chucked his janitor's gear into a Dumpster. They weren't much use to him anymore; the back wheels of the plastic pail had broken off and the mop's handle had cracked in half. The large man strode out of the alley, keeping his mop-covered head down, and darted toward the first cab he saw. He opened the yellow door and slid inside. "Drive, cabbie," he growled, anxiously peering behind him as police sirens grew closer.

"Off duty!" the driver said in a thick accent, before returning to his cell phone.

The very large man reached out a very large hand and snapped the cab driver's phone shut in one smooth gesture.

"Hey! What do you think—" The cab driver broke off as he glimpsed the giant in the back seat, his head covered in strange, white, rope-like dreadlocks, which smelled oddly of disinfectant. "Anywhere you want to go, my friend! Anywhere you want to go!"

"Take me to the Holland Tunnel." The large

man looked out the rear window toward the wail of sirens. "And step on it!"

The cab careened down FDR Drive like a yellow bullet.

"Faster," growled the very large man.

"I'm going as fast as I can possibly go without getting pulled over. You know, my friend, I am sensing you have a lot of unresolved anger. Maybe you should consider getting a massage or taking a yoga class?"

The very large man didn't reply. He was almost as cramped and uncomfortable in the tiny cab as he had been in his tiny cell, the top of his head making a small dent in the ceiling.

"Tell me, why are you in such a hurry, my friend?"

"I've gotta meeting." The very large man glanced out the rear window at the East Side traffic; there didn't seem to be any police cars. He leaned back against the seat, finally relaxing. "A real important meeting."

A little while later, the cab entered the dark mouth of the Holland tunnel.

"Excuse me, my friend," called the cab driver. "But after we pass through the tunnel, where do you want me to go?"

The very large man didn't reply. He stared out his window, watching the tiled walls whiz by. "Slow down!" he barked. His face was nearly mashed against the window-pane, he was studying the tunnel walls so intently. "Drive a little more, just a little, and then let me out."

"Let you out?" the driver repeated in disbelief. "You are in the middle of an *underwater* tunnel!"

"I said, LET ME OUT!" The cab screeched to a halt, nearly causing a catastrophic pile-up as cars honked and drivers yelled out angrily. As the large man bolted out of the side door, the cab peeled away.

"You have a screw loose, my friend," the cab driver called out the window, one finger circling his temple. "You are in the middle of an underwater tunnel! Where are you going to go?!"

The very large man walked, hunched over, close to the tunnel wall, examining the tiles, as cars whizzed by. Then he saw it. A small etching of a hawk, a cheetah, and a crocodile. The very large man lifted a very large hand and knocked three long knocks and three short ones. The etching began to spin, slowly at first and then faster. The large man leaned against the wall. And one moment he was an odd man leaning against a wall of the Holland Tunnel, and the next moment he was gone, the wall quickly slipping back into place as if it had never moved at all.

CHAPTER 3

The Juvenile Delinquent

There was a school of angry sharks, and they were swimming in Anna's stomach. At least that's what it felt like as she stared up at the gold plaque on the perfectly polished wooden door:

Thaddeus T. Rollins
PRINCIPAL

Anna had never been sent to the principal's office before. Sure, she had seen Mr. Rollins at school assemblies, with his tailored suit and neatly brushed hair, but she had never actually talked with him alone before. Anna lifted a fist to knock—

"He's in there with some people. Three other people. So that would be a total of four people to be exact."

Anna turned around to find Simon Spektor sitting on a bench against the wall bent over a small handheld video game.

"Oh." She slumped down next to him. "Are you in trouble too?"

Simon shook his head. "No." He took a tissue from a large box by his side and noisily blew his nose. "I've got to see Dr. Oshinko. My ears have been hurting me; I have redness and swelling, this morning I could've sworn I had a fever, and now I feel a headache coming on. I think I might have Mastoiditis. I'm just dropping off my doctor's note."

Simon Spektor had straight dark hair that lay flat around his head like a bowl, extra-thick glasses, and a clip-on bowtie that his parents no doubt thought was cute but had no clue that something like that would ruin their son's social life. Not that Simon even had a social life that Anna knew of. Yes, he was technically in her grade, but he was always absent because he was sick, and always missing class to visit some sort of doctor.

"Why are you visiting the principal?" Simon asked in his nasal voice. A small mountain of crumpled, snot-filled tissues was beginning to pile up on the floor beneath him.

"It's a long story." Anna sighed. "Story of my life, actually. Don't worry, I won't bore you with the details."

Simon shrugged and bent back over his game.

Suddenly the door opened with a creak, and Thaddeus T. Rollins stepped out, followed by three police officers.

"Well, if you see anything suspicious, be sure to call the precinct right away!" one of the police officers was saying.

"Yes. Yes." Mr. Rollins clasped his well-manicured hands together. "I'm sure if I see a seven-foot-tall, seething criminal sitting in one of our classrooms, I will be sure to call the police!"

"This is no joke, Mr. Rollins. This is the biggest jail-break in a decade! Donny 'the Meatball' Fratelli is the most dangerous hitman there is."

"Killed a guy with a spoon once!" Another officer interjected.

"*A spoon?*" Mr. Rollins repeated, dumbfounded.

"Yup! Gutted the poor guy. Scooped out his insides like it was frozen yogurt!"

Anna gulped, grabbing the seat of the bench with white knuckles.

"Yes, well, I'm sure everyone here at Bendox is quite safe." Mr. Rollins sounded nervous now. "I mean, this is a school. An excellent school, at that! What interest would a criminal have here?"

"We got a tip-off. It probably has nothing to do with any of the kids, but kids have parents, Mr. Rollins. Some kid's parents could be caught up in some bad business. Or a teacher."

Mr. Rollins's face blanched. "But that's not possible. One of the parents—one of our teachers—involved with a killer—"

A loud trumpet-like blowing interrupted them. The officers and Mr. Rollins turned to look at Simon Spektor as he wiped his nose and dug into a nostril after a booger.

"Well, we should be going," said the officer, eyeing Anna and Simon. "Just remember, this guy's got no Jiminy Cricket on his shoulder, if you know what I mean."

Anna watched the officers disappear down the long hallway, wishing they would stay, especially if a dangerous criminal was on the loose. And if they stayed, maybe she wouldn't have to talk to the principal.

"What is it now, Simon?" Thaddeus T. Rollins asked, impatiently.

Simon hopped down from the bench into his pile of tissues. "I've got a doctor's appointment," he said in his nasal voice, holding out a stained note.

"Of course you do." Mr. Rollins disdainfully took hold of the note with two of his fingers. "Now run along."

Grabbing his large box of tissues, Simon threw Anna a weak smile before heading down the hallway.

"And why aren't you in class, filling your young mind with new ideas?" Mr. Rollins crossed his arms and stared down at Anna.

Anna handed him the note from Ms. Musashi.

"Hmm," he said, reading it. "This is very serious business, Miss Smudge. It says here you attacked the Pierce boy, pulling his hair and biting—"

"I didn't bite him!" Anna protested.

Thaddeus T. Rollins glared at her from over his gold-rimmed spectacles. "Miss Smudge, I do not care whether you bit Mr. Pierce, hit Mr. Pierce, or stole Mr. Pierce's lunch money! The point is that none of this behavior is tolerated at the Bendox School of Excellence. Here at Bendox, we strive for a higher standard of education."

Anna stared down at her feet.

"I will give you one warning, Miss Smudge, and only

one, and if this happens again I will be forced to call your parents."

So he wasn't going to call her parents. Anna breathed a sigh of relief.

"So what do you have to say for yourself, young lady?"

Anna just stared at the principal, who was as perfectly polished as his door. What did he want her to say, that Jacob was a royal jerk?

"Miss Smudge, are you going to apologize to Jacob Pierce personally?"

A surge of anger hit Anna, and before she could stop herself she blurted, "I won't apologize to *him!* I won't! I wish I did bite him! He deserved it!"

Just as the angry words had left her mouth, Anna wished she could gather them all back and swallow them up. Worried, she looked at the group of police officers, who were lounging near the front door. Would Mr. Rollins call them back to arrest her? Was she now a juvenile delinquent? She glanced back up at the principal. He looked as if he had swallowed a pigeon.

"You will go talk with the guidance counselor now! Maybe she can get to the root of your problem. Go!"

Anna snatched the note and stormed down the hall. She was fed up—with her teachers, with Mr. Rollins, and now the stupid guidance counselor. Just another grown-up who would yap and yap and yap and not even hear what she had to say! Anna had glimpsed the guidance counselor a couple of times in the cafeteria. She was a pinched woman who looked as if she had been sucking on lemons all year.

.•.

Just as Anna was about to knock on the guidance coun-selor's door, a woman with blonde curly hair backed out of the room. "See you tomorrow at eight, sis. Just don't forget what happened the last time you tried to make meatloaf!" The woman turned and nearly ran right into Anna. "AHHK!!"

Anna was surprised to see that it was her art teacher, Mrs. Summer. "Don't frighten me like that, little one!" squeaked the shaken woman. She adjusted her colorful scarf fretfully, as if she were getting hot flashes. Then Mrs. Summer patted Anna on the head like a dog before escap-ing down the hall.

Anna sighed and stepped inside the room only to find a teen-aged girl perched atop a stepladder. The girl cheerfully waved before jumping down to the floor.

"I just hung it! Watcha think?"

Anna peered up at the weird painting that looked like someone had eaten their spaghetti dinner over a white canvas. "It's crooked."

"Yeah," the girl said, chin in hand, but then her face brightened. "But not if you look at it like this!" She tilted her head to the left. "Now it's perfect!" And she let loose a hearty laugh. Anna couldn't help but smile a little.

"So did Thaddeus send you my way?"

"Yeah. I'm supposed to talk to the guidance counselor because I'm such a juvenile delinquent."

"You don't seem like a juvenile delinquent. You look like someone made you very angry, but I don't think I'd categorize you as a criminal yet!"

"Well, everyone else thinks so. Ms. Musashi, Principal Rollins, and I bet the guidance counselor, Old Sourpuss—" She stopped abruptly.

"What?" the girl said with a laugh. "What were you going to say?"

"Oh, nothing. You're probably her daughter, so I shouldn't say anything."

"Actually, I'm the new guidance counselor."

Anna stared at her. How could that be? This girl was so young, and she didn't act like a teacher, or even a grown-up for that matter.

"I know, I know," the girl said with a laugh. "I look about fifteen, but I guarantee you I'm not. I got my masters degree in psychology at Columbia. I've always looked really young for my age. But I'm cool with it now."

"Anyway," the girl continued with a lopsided grin. "I haven't even introduced myself. I'm Ms. Sinclair."

"I'm Anna. So, if you're the new guidance counselor...I should talk to you?"

"I guess so. Why don't you have a seat in my office," Ms. Sinclair said with a smile, motioning to a large pillow on the floor. To Anna's complete surprise, Ms. Sinclair plopped down on another pillow next to her and crossed her legs. "So, what's up? Is there anything in particular you'd like to talk about?"

"Don't you want to read this first?" Anna held out Ms. Musashi's note. Ms. Sinclair took it and stuffed it into one of her back pockets.

"I'd like to hear *you* tell me what happened."

Anna looked at Ms. Sinclair, a little shocked. Most grown-ups usually started lecturing right away or asked questions as if their minds were already made up, so what was the use in talking? But Anna looked at the young woman sitting across from her and, for the first time, really felt like...well, felt like telling her everything.

She talked about being the slowest person in New York City, of having the nickname Sludge; she talked about how rarely she saw her parents. She even mentioned how Rachel got her feelings hurt and that she didn't know what to do to help. It all seemed to pour out of her like a cool pitcher of lemonade, making her feel refreshed afterward. All the while, Ms. Sinclair sat across from Anna in silence. In fact, she didn't move an inch the whole time... but her eyes. It was as if Anna could see everything she was telling Ms. Sinclair reflected back in her eyes. And it made Anna feel... good.

When Anna finally got to Jacob Pierce, she could feel her cheeks get hot again, just describing the injustice of it all.

"And now I'm here," she exclaimed, clapping her hands on her lap, a little embarrassed at how long she had been talking for. Who knew she had so much to say?

"Wow. That's quite a time you've had," Ms. Sinclair said with a sympathetic smile. "Anna, I listened to everything you said, but the most interesting part for me was when you described yourself as slow. How do you mean?"

"I'm just slow," Anna sighed. "I'm a sludge."

"But *why* do you think you're slow?"

Anna thought for a long moment, first thinking back to her morning, and then to her life in general. "Well, I guess ever since I was very little, I liked to take my time doing things. Like after I learned to tie my shoes. It wasn't that I couldn't tie them quickly. It was that it was something new, and I enjoyed doing it. I wanted to make sure that I did every step correctly. You know, making the two big loops just right. I never thought of myself as being slow. It just seemed that everyone else around me was always in such a hurry."

Anna paused, thinking about the streams of people pouring through the city streets at rush hour. "I mean if you're always running around, hurrying to get on to the next thing, you're not really doing anything at all. You're just hurrying."

Anna stopped. Ms. Sinclair had a weird expression on her face. "What?" she said, feeling a little self-conscious. "Am I weirding you out?"

"Not at all. I just think what you said is very wise."

"For my age?"

"For *any* age." Ms. Sinclair sat on her cushion and thought, her pretty face puckered into an intense expression. "Tell me something, Anna. When everyone in New York is hurrying through life, what do you think they might be missing?"

"I don't know," Anna said, slowly turning the question

over in her mind. "A lot of things...little things...it's like they're too busy racing around to really notice stuff."

Ms. Sinclair nodded thoughtfully. "When people are always rushing, they might hear what you say, but they're not really *listening*. Their minds are too full to take in what you're really saying, so they miss out on the details."

"Yes! Exactly!"

"Anna," Ms. Sinclair continued, a warm smile spreading across her face. "You say you're slow, but I think you have a very special gift. What you think is your fault, I think is your biggest asset. It sets you apart from everyone else."

Anna looked at Ms. Sinclair, puzzled. "You mean I'm not really slow?"

"Anna, you simply take your time. You have the ability to *really* stop and listen. You see things that others don't because they're too busy to notice."

Anna sat on her cushion thinking while Ms. Sinclair continued.

"Earlier, you talked about how lousy it feels when no one listens to you. And then you mentioned your friend who got her feelings hurt. If you wanted to, I bet you could help people like her. It sounds like you want to."

"But how?"

"Sometimes people just need someone to listen, to really hear them. And maybe point things out that they were too upset to notice."

"Like you do," Anna said softly. "So, I could be like you. I could be like a shrink!"

Ms. Sinclair laughed a deep warm laugh. "Yes. Yes, I guess you could be a therapist if you wanted to."

All of a sudden, Anna felt like crying, but she didn't know why since she felt so happy. She wasn't just a Sludge! She was going to be a shrink! She was going to help other people like Ms. Sinclair had helped her.

Anna glanced up at Ms. Sinclair, suddenly uneasy. "You won't tell anyone everything that I told you today, will you?"

Ms. Sinclair smiled reassuringly. "No, I won't, Anna. In therapy there is something called confidentiality, meaning that whatever a patient says stays strictly between the therapist and the patient."

"Like a secret?"

"Yes, a secret. No matter how embarrassing or funny or horrible, the therapist can *never* repeat what a patient tells them. Or reveal who that patient is."

Suddenly, there was a knock on the door, and Thaddeus T. Rollins stuck his neatly brushed head into the room. "Excuse me, am I interrupting? Why, Miss Smudge, are you still here?"

"We were just finishing up," said Ms. Sinclair.

"Oh, very good then." Mr. Rollins stepped into the room. "I called the girl's parents. I left a message on a gentleman's machine—Her father, I presume."

Anna felt the sharks circling once again. *Principal Rollins had left a message on her father's answering machine!*

"So, Miss Smudge, anything you'd like to say to make your situation any *worse?*" Mr. Rollins asked glibly.

Anna shook her head, thinking it best to remain silent.

But what she didn't know was that the situation was getting worse by the minute. Someone else was standing outside, quiet as a shadow, ear pressed to the small crack in the door...listening.

Donny 'the Meatball' Fratelli," said a voice as smooth as silk. "It's so nice of you to drop by. Take a seat. We were just getting started."

The very large man carefully tiptoed into the room attached to the Holland Tunnel, anxiously looking down at his feet because it looked like he was stepping on...nothing.

"Now, Mr. Fratelli, there's no need to worry. You know the glass this room is made from is the strongest in the world. After all, I manufacture it!"

Nervous laughter filled the room as the large man took an empty seat at a long glass table in the center of the glass room. Familiar faces of famous criminals, scientists and businessmen filled the other seats, and at the very head of the glass table sat the only thing in the entire room that you couldn't see through—a dark partition. Behind it was Mr. Who.

"Gentlemen," said the silky voice. "Shall we talk business?"

The glass room creaked and groaned from the pressure of the Hudson River on all sides.

The large man couldn't help but wonder what would happen if one of the walls cracked...just a little.

"I need to win this government shipping contract, gentlemen. I need the army to use one of my ships to transport that cargo."

Dr. LeGrande, an impeccably dressed black man, cleared his throat. He was very handsome except for one milky-white eye, which glistened blankly in the dim light. "If you don't mind my asking Mr. Who, what exactly is the government moving?"

Everyone in the room leaned forward, eager to hear the answer.

"They are moving something that I want," snapped the voice. "That's all you need to know. Now tell me, what is our status on this project?"

With trembling hands, Dr. LeGrande fumbled through a small pile of papers. "Well, Mr. Who, we placed a bid, but unfortunately so did Mr. Smudge's shipping company."

"NO," boomed the voice.

"Um, yes, sir," Dr. LeGrande replied. "And Mr. Smudge has an excellent reputation. His ships are superior to ours. I'm afraid we can't compete with someone like him. It's unlikely we'll win this job."

There was a silence. Just the moan of the Hudson River. Suddenly a buzzer sounded, and the glass seat Dr. LeGrande sat in sunk down into the glass floor, taking Dr. LeGrande with it. When it rose back up again, the seat was empty. There was just the sound of frantic banging as Dr. LeGrande desperately knocked against the underside of the glass floor, the cold water of the Hudson swirling around him...and then there was no sound at all.

"Does anyone else want to tell me that something cannot be done?" asked the silky voice.

No one answered.

"The government has something that belongs to me and I intend to get it back! Mr. Fratelli, are you available?"

"Sure," the large man replied. "I'm free. Free as a bird."

"Good. I need you to run a small errand with me tonight. Also, contact Mr. Smudge immediately, and let him know that it is in his very best interest to retract his bid and let us win this shipping contract."

"Should I kill him, boss?"

There was another silence.

"No," Mr. Who said finally. "We should call him first. Mr. Smudge should know who he's competing with."

The very large man nodded.

"And Mr. Fratelli, you might want to do something... with your hair."

The large man reached up, suddenly remembering the mop on his head, and nodded.

The Answering Machine

"Anna. Hey, Anna!"

Anna turned to see a frantic-looking Quenton pushing his way through the crowd in the school foyer. "What took so long? You missed lunch!" He held out a large lump wrapped in foil. "It was sloppy joes. And man, the chefs here have no idea how to season meat. So I sautéed some onions and peppers in the teachers' lounge and added them for flavor."

"Thanks, Quenton." Starved, Anna unwrapped her lunch and ate as they walked.

Outside, kids crowded the sidewalk, fumbling for their Metrocards to pay for the subway, clustered in groups, and talking wildly among themselves.

"Anna, oh my gosh!" Rachel exclaimed, galloping over, her blondish braids swinging wildly. "I almost called my mom! You took longer than the N train! What did Principal Rollins say?"

Anna bit her lip, her eyes filling with fear. "You guys, Mr. Rollins called my father. He left a message on his answering machine."

"Oh no," moaned Quenton. "Anna, your dad is going to hit the roof."

"That's it!" Rachel cut in. "When my mom gets here, I'm telling her! She'll know what to do. We'll have to do some research. I don't know if she's handled any cases like this before, but—"

"This is not a sexual harassment case, Rachel!" Quenton interrupted. "Anna does not need legal representation. What she needs to do is get home before her father, sneak into his study, and erase that message before anyone hears it."

"Um, guys," Anna gulped. "I don't know."

But Rachel nodded her head vigorously. "I think you're right, Quenton. Anna is going to be in a world of trouble if she doesn't. Besides, this is Anna Smudge we're talking about. It's not like she bites people all the time."

"I didn't bite him," Anna muttered.

"Yeah! Anna doesn't deserve to get into trouble. It was all Pierce's fault. That caveman deserved to be bitten!"

"I didn't bite him."

Finally, it was all agreed on. Anna would erase the message when she got home.

"So, Anna, I hope you learned a lesson for biting my cousin."

Anna turned to find Roselyn clad in a camelhair coat straight from the display window of Bergdorf's. She was about to say again that she didn't bite anyone, but thought better of it and kept her mouth shut.

"Well, I guess money doesn't buy class. Come on, Amy!"

Roselyn turned with an impatient swoosh of her coat, followed close behind by an uncertain Amy Lerner.

A cherry-red Viper convertible screeched to the curb, cutting off a bike messenger, who tumbled over his handlebars and onto the concrete. Jacob's dad, dressed in dark sunglasses and leather, climbed out of the car, screaming and kicking his feet at the messenger's mangled bike.

"Jeez, looks like he's got a temper on him," muttered Rachel. "Like father, like son, eh?"

"I'm telling you, old Pierce is bad news," said Quenton.

Watching Mr. Pierce reminded Anna of something. "Hey, did you guys know that there were cops in Mr. Rollins's office today? They said that a parent or teacher might be involved with this dangerous escaped criminal."

"Well there you go, Anna. You don't have to look much further than him." Quenton gestured to Mr. Pierce, who was now yapping on his cell like he was talking to the President. He motioned for Jacob and Roselyn to hop in, and the car sped away toward Lexington Avenue. Amy, now alone, retreated behind one of the school's planters, looking like a timid rabbit, her eyes nervously darting about.

Quenton turned to Anna with a look of dread. "My dad's almost here."

Quenton was mixed race. His mom was black, and his dad was a small, white, Jewish man who owned a tiny lighting store in midtown called *All Lit Up!* Mr. Cohen drove around in a van covered with lightbulbs to advertise the shop. Quenton always got embarrassed when his dad picked them up. Anna thought he was very lucky. She would have loved for her father to pick her up…just once.

"Please be late, Dad! Please be late!" Quenton muttered. Of course, at that moment, Quenton's dad pulled up in his "Light Mobile."

"Hi, kids!" he said as he got out of the van.

"Hi, Mr. Cohen!" Anna said.

"Dad, what are you doing?" Quenton hissed, nervously looking around as people on the sidewalk stopped to gawk at the Light Mobile. "Let us get in so we can go home. Everyone's staring!"

"Great!" Mr. Cohen said, tipping his lightbulb-covered hat as people walked by. "It'll be great advertisement for the store."

"Daaad!" Quenton whined.

"Alrighty!" Mr. Cohen said, heading around to the passenger seat. "Let me just move some stuff."

After a couple minutes of grappling with blinking lampshades, throw pillows with strings of lights hanging off the edges and illuminated Converse sneakers, among other contraptions, Mr. Cohen resurfaced, looking like a mild tornado had just hit. "OK! Hop in kids!"

Quenton and Anna squashed together in the back seat. Quenton ducked down so no one could recognize him. Anna clutched a pile of psychology books Ms. Sinclair had given her and smiled. But her smile slowly faded as she remembered what she had to do when she got home.

"Quenton," she whispered. "Quenton, I don't know if I can do it. I'm just not sure."

CHAPTER 4

"Do what?"

"You know. Sneak into my father's study, erase Principal Rollins's message. Isn't that lying?"

"Lying?" Quenton said. "No, that's just *hiding* the truth. Lying is when you're *asked* about something and you say something that's not true."

"Oh," Anna said, growing more confused as the conversation went on.

"You'd just better hope nobody asks you about it."

"Why?"

"Because *then* you'd be lying."

Anna stood in front of the tall wood-paneled doors of her father's study and peered into the vast room. This was the one room in the apartment that was off-limits to her. Towering glass-enclosed bookcases filled with model ships lined the walls. Oriental rugs covered the floor. And at the far end of the room—in front of giant windows framed by sweeping velvet curtains—sat her father's antique mahogany desk.

Anna took a deep breath and started the long walk, trying to make as little sound as possible. She could see the red blinking light of her father's answering machine. She could hear the maid scurrying around in the other room, her footsteps growing louder and closer. There was a loud creak just outside the door...

Anna froze. She was standing smack in the center of the enormous room with no place to hide. She held her breath, knowing she was caught……but nothing happened. The maid's footsteps grew softer and farther away, and then there was silence once again.

Her heart racing, Anna tiptoed over to the desk, eager to get it over with. But the answering machine displayed the number 2 in its little window. Her father had *two* new messages. How would she know which one was from Thaddeus T. Rollins? She couldn't play them out loud; the maid would surely hear.

Biting her lip, Anna looked around, trying to find an answer…and then her gaze fell on a gold frame. It was an old photograph of her and her father at the duck pond in Central Park. She remembered when he used to take her there on Saturdays. Anna studied the man in the picture. He seemed so different, so young, or maybe it was that he was laughing. And the way he was looking at the tiny girl in the picture…at her. It was with such pride!

But that was a long, long time ago.

Anna felt the sting of tears and brushed them away with the back of her sleeve. She reached out a trembling hand and, with two quick taps, erased both messages from the answering machine.

A Mysterious Phone Call

A swirl of regret enfolded Anna as she stared at the little window on her father's answering machine, which now read 0. Whose message had she erased? There was a low rumble, and Anna quickly scrambled out into the marble foyer just as the elevator door opened and out stepped her parents.

"Well hello, pumpkin!" Mr. Smudge said, walking toward his study.

"Anna, did you just get in?" Mrs. Smudge asked, unwrapping a silk scarf from her neck.

Anna just stood there frozen, like a deer in headlights. She could feel her heart sink to the very bottom of her stomach, mingling with the sloppy joe and sautéed veggies she had gulped down for lunch.

"Anna, honey, are you coming up?"

Anna took one last glance at her father's study and then followed her mother up the stairs and into her bedroom.

Anna watched as her mother brushed out her hair. She was so pretty. It was hard to believe that she was her mother. She looked like she should be the mother of someone like Roselyn Pierce, with her perfectly curled hair and painted nails.

"So where are we going for dinner tonight?" Anna wrung her hands hopefully. "Quenton said there's a really great sushi place we should try and—"

"Oh, sweetie, your father and I have a business dinner."

"Again?"

"I'm afraid so," Anna's mother answered absentmindedly as she clipped on a pair of dressy earrings. "Your father has placed a bid on a very important job. If he wins, the government will use one of your father's ships to transport a special container for the army."

"What's in the container?"

Anna's mother disappeared into the bathroom. "It's top secret. Even your father doesn't know. So, I can't discuss it."

Anna wandered back downstairs and flipped on the radio in the kitchen.

> Donny "the Meatball" Fratelli
> escaped from Harlem Prison earlier
> today while posing as a janitor. He
> then caused the strangest police
> chase in history as he made his get-
> away riding in a wheeled mop bucket.

A chill went up Anna's spine like a skittering spider. She had seen him! She had seen him in the cab on her way to school this morning! If only she had seen what he looked like.

Authorities are urging the public to be on a steady watch. Though Fratelli has claimed to have killed more people than he can count on both hands, there is much speculation as to whether he can count at all—

"Well, we're off, pumpkin," Mr. Smudge said.

"Have a good night, sweetheart," said Mrs. Smudge. "Perhaps we'll see you in the morning."

Probably not, Anna thought glumly as her parents gave her a quick peck on the cheek. Then they were out the door, followed only by the click, click of their dress shoes and the low rumble of the elevator.

Anna flicked the radio off. Listening to the news was giving her the creeps. Especially after hearing those cops talk to Principal Rollins at Bendox that afternoon. Instead, Anna spread her new psychology books out on the table and began to pour through them one-by-one. She remembered Ms. Sinclair's warm smile and her easy-going laugh. As she read, she thought about how Ms. Sinclair had listened, the questions she had asked and the things she pointed out to make Anna feel so good.

Just then, the telephone rang. Anna reached for the cordless. "Hello?"

There was some hushed whispering on the other end.

"Hello?" Anna said, a bit louder. "This is Anna, who is this?"

"*I know what you did,*" a strange-sounding voice said.

"Who is this? Are you looking to speak with my father, because he has a separate business line. I could—"

"*I'm speaking to you, Anna!*"

Anna crinkled her brow. "Quenton, is that you? And why does your voice sound so weird?"

"*No,*" the voice crackled mechanically. There was a pause, and then some whispers. Anna strained her ears to hear. Then the voice sounded once again.

"*I know you erased the message from your father's answering machine.*"

Anna clutched the table with white knuckles. "How did you know that? Who is this? What do you want?"

"*I'll be in touch soon.*"

There was a click, and the dial tone sounded.

It was one of those damp and chilly nights when the city seemed darker than usual. Mysterious black shadows rose and fell like they belonged to the Boogeyman, but the large man strode right by them fearlessly. After all, he already knew the Boogeyman. He worked for him.

When the large man reached the sleek car with black windows he glanced around warily and then climbed into the front seat.

"Good evening, Mr. Fratelli," said the voice as smooth as silk.

"Hey, Mr. Who." The large man shifted awkwardly in the driver's seat, took a deep breath, and finally looked at his rearview mirror. But he couldn't see Mr. Who. There was a thick, dark partition dividing the front and back seat.

"Drive me to the address posted on the windshield," ordered the voice. "When we get there, I need you to escort the woman to the backseat of this car so that I can have a chat with her."

"You're going to talk to her face-to-face?" the large man asked, feeling the creepy-crawlies.

"Yes, I am. And afterward she will give me whatever I want."

They drove in silence. The large man wanted to turn on the radio, but he wasn't sure what kind of music Mr. Who liked, and he didn't feel like getting killed over a bad song.

"Mr. Fratelli," inquired the silky voice. "Did you get in touch with Mr. Smudge?"

"Yes, Mr. Who, sir. I called earlier and left a message on his answering machine."

"Good."

The large man pulled over at the curb, triple-checking the address to make sure it was correct before climbing out and knocking on a large door. A woman with curly blonde hair, a large colorful scarf and an apron smeared with paint answered. She had a bright smile on her face, which slowly crumpled as she looked up...and then up a little higher at the very large man.

"No...no, no, nononono," she rattled off in uncontrollable fright. "Please, not one of you guys again. Please," she choked, "I've already told you I can't. I won't!" The woman moved to shut the door. "I-I have to go now."

But the large man wasn't done yet. He shoved his very large shoe in the way. The woman jumped back and squeaked like a trapped mouse.

The large man smiled. He always liked this part. "My boss, Mr. Who, is here."

"M-Mr. Who?" the woman stuttered in disbelief. "B-But he's not real."

Grabbing a chunk of curly blonde hair in case she started running, the large man escorted the woman over to the car. She was saying something, but the large man didn't really pay attention. They all blabbered and blubbered when the time came. It was in the job description.

The large man opened the door to a pitch-black backseat and shoved the woman inside. Then he shut the door and waited. The large man paced around, examining the darkness. He thought he saw a sneaker peeking out from behind a couple garbage bins and maybe even a backpack, but then he shrugged. Rats in this city grew to be all sizes and shapes.

Suddenly the light in the backseat of the car flicked on, and the woman began to scream: "YOU! IT'S YOU! NO! IT CAN'T BE! IT CAN'T BE! NO! NOOOOOOOOO!

The woman screamed frantically, like a person awakening in their worst nightmare. And the pair of sneakers hiding behind the garbage bins took off down the block, running as fast as they could.

CHAPTER 6

Eggs Over Easy with a Side of Blackmail

Anna awoke in the morning with a sinking feeling in the pit of her stomach. She vaguely remembered doing something wrong. As she walked by the closed door of her father's study it all came tumbling back to her like a bad dream—the two messages she had erased, and that horrible phone call afterward.

On the subway, Anna peered around at all the other dazed New Yorkers clutching their coffee cups. Someone out there knew what she had done. Someone...

When Anna entered the large red doors of Bendox, she was hunched over into a small ball of worry. Things could not get any worse, she thought as she opened her locker. And that's when a piece of paper fluttered down from one of the slots.

Smudge:
If you want to live a long life and not have your parents disown you, you'll follow these directions:
Do two sets of homework for the

rest of the week. Make sure that each one is written in handwriting different from your own.

Leave the homework under the currency exchange booth, east of the clock in Grand Central Station. The drop must be made before 7:00 a.m. !

If the homework is not there by that time, or you attempt to hide out and watch, your parents will find out what you did!

— Anonymous

"And things just got worse," Anna mumbled, shoving the note into her pocket. Just then, the front doors opened and Quenton sauntered in.

"What's up? You're early for, like, the first time ever!"

Anna just looked at him, her face ashen.

"What's wrong?" Quenton examined her closely. Then he quickly held up a hand. "Wait! Tell me at Café Pacella. We have half an hour before first period, and I've been craving smoked salmon and crème fraîche like you wouldn't believe."

.•.

CLANK! The waitress dropped a fancy dish in front of Quenton, and some plain eggs in front of Anna. Quenton insisted on having fresh pepper. And as Anna poured a pool of ketchup on her plate, he eyed her quizzically.

"That's a sin. I'm telling you, Anna, ketchup is a sad excuse for a condiment."

Anna rolled her eyes and smacked the crumbled black-mail note on the table. *"This* was in my locker."

Quenton's raised his eyebrows as he scanned the page. "Jeez, Anna!"

"I know," Anna replied softly. "First I got this mysterious phone call last night, and now this..." She shook her head. "I'm pretty sure it's Jacob."

Quenton inspected the note again, doubtful. "I don't think so. Jacob's a major freak, but I don't think he's behind this."

"But you said that Ms. Musashi sent him to the nurse after I left. He could have followed me to Rollins's office and found out about the message. Or he could have heard us talking after school."

Quenton looked skeptical. "Yeah, but think about it. Jacob lives all the way on the Upper West Side. Why would he have you drop the homework off at Grand Central Station when it's completely out of the way for him? Why not pick a drop closer to him? It just doesn't add up."

"Of course it adds up! You saw him yesterday—calling me Sludge, making faces at me...tripping me in math class, for crying out loud!"

"That's what he always does. Look, Anna." Quenton smoothed the note out. "This note is neatly written. There are no spelling mistakes that I can see. Nothing. It's perfect. Jacob Pierce isn't smart enough to pull something like this off. He's just a stupid bully!"

"No, he's a turd," Clea Rodriguez said, standing over their table.

"Um, excuse me?" Anna looked behind her just to make sure Clea was talking to them...because Clea Rodriguez never talked to anyone. Clea was the shortest kid in their grade but also the scariest. She wore black leather, chains and a camera around her neck, and she stalked the school hallways with her headphones cranked all the way up.

"A turd," Clea repeated. "You know, a disgusting piece of dung. That's what Jacob Pierce is."

Anna just nodded.

"You did good yesterday. Biting him. I would have just—" BANG! Clea slammed a leather-gloved fist on the tabletop, making Anna's ketchup splatter all over the place like blood. Then she quickly snapped a picture of them before storming out the door.

"Oh my God, she talked to you!" Quenton gawked. "Even better, she called Jacob a little brown turd! You should bite people more often."

"How many times do I have to say it? I did not bite Jacob!" Anna buried her face in her hands. "This cannot be happening to me! Like being eleven and having to take gym isn't hard enough?"

"Mmm. Now that's what I'm talking about!" Quenton patted his mouth with his napkin. "Think I have time for another order?"

"Time?" Anna repeated, suddenly looking up at the clock above their booth. "Quenton, we have to go! Art class is starting now."

Anna stressed aloud as they ran the block back to Bendox. She just could not be late for another class. What she needed was a really good excuse. She was already in so much trouble without being late again.

"Relax, Anna," Quenton said nonchalantly as they scurried down the stairs toward the art studio. "It's just stupid Mrs. Summer. That lady is such a flake, you could put her in a bowl, pour milk over her, and eat her for breakfast—"

Quenton broke off as he smacked right into a police officer. Anna grinded to a stop right in back of Quenton.

"Um, sorry, officer," Quenton muttered. "We just have to get to art class through that door there…" He trailed off as he noticed all the other police officers and a small crowd of scared-looking kindergarteners huddled in a corner.

"What's going on?"

"Kid, you better stand over here." The officer guided Anna and Quenton over to a wall lined with other kids from their grade. And then the screaming started.

"HE'S REAL! I'M TELLING YOU, HE'S REAL! WHY WON'T YOU BELIEVE ME? I SAW HIM!"

Anna sucked in a breath as a group of men in white jackets and a couple police officers escorted Mrs. Summer, their art teacher, from the art studio. Mrs. Summer was stuffed into a straightjacket, her blonde curly hair was streaked with orange and green paint, her face was the color of a tomato, and her eyes darted around like a wild animal as she screamed at the top of her lungs.

"HE EXISTS! I SAW HIM! HIM AND THE MAN

WITH THE PURPLE SHOES! THEY CAME TO ME! HE THREATENED TO KILL MY STUDENTS! HE SAID HE'D FINGER-PAINT WITH THEIR BLOOD!"

Suddenly Mrs. Summer broke free and began to race around the hallway in a circle, her eyes wild. "I KNOW, CHILDREN! I KNOW!" She stopped in front of Anna. Drool dribbled down her chin. "I KNOW WHO **WHO** IS."

And then the officers tackled Mrs. Summer and shuffled her up the stairs.

CHAPTER 7

Big Mouth

"She finally cracked. Just like an Easter egg."

"Stop it, Quenton," Rachel scolded. "That's not nice."

Anna, Quenton, and Rachel sat in an empty classroom on a bunch of clumped-together desks as police officers and teachers handled the ensuing chaos in the outside hallway.

"I'm just stating the obvious," Quenton continued. "Our art teacher has gone insane. I mean, Mrs. Summer's always been a little loopy. But now she's nuttier than those almond cookies I made last week. I mean, 'I know who *who* is?' What is she an owl? What does that even mean?"

"Obviously she was talking about Mr. Who," Rachel said matter-of-factly.

"Mr. Who?!" Anna gasped at the mention of the name.

"Give me a break, you guys," Quenton snorted. "Mr. Who doesn't really exist. He's like this myth. Like the Boogeyman or something."

"He's real!" Rachel insisted. "Just because no one's ever seen his face doesn't mean he doesn't exist."

"Nah, it's all a big conspiracy," Quenton retorted. "It's just something the government made up as an excuse for why they can't cut down on crime. They say it's because this mysterious, non-existent guy, Mr. Who, runs all of these crime organizations all over the world. Total fluff, if you ask me."

Rachel was indignant. "Quenton, this is serious! Don't you see? Mrs. Summer *saw* Mr. Who! That's what she was trying to tell us."

"OK, so let's say he *is* real. Which he's not. What would a big-time criminal mastermind like Mr. Who want with an art teacher?"

Rachel opened her mouth but then closed it, stumped.

"And," Quenton continued, "let's say Mrs. Summer did see Mr. Who. Why would it drive her bonkers?"

"Well, Mrs. Summer lost it every time she saw a bug. She wasn't exactly stable, if you know what I mean."

Anna sighed and glanced around the classroom, which was slowly filling up with sixth-graders. That's when she noticed Todd Brecken-Bayer sitting nearby, clenching a soccer ball with white knuckles. Surprisingly, he was by himself, quietly listening to their conversation, a deeply disturbed expression in his crystal-blue eyes.

"Um, let's change the subject," Anna said abruptly. "This is kind of upsetting. So, what else is going on in the world, Rachel?"

"Well, did you guys hear about the car bombing in

Kabul?" Rachel chirped. "Just awful! Oh, and a new health report says that if you want to stay healthy, you need to exercise for at least an hour a day."

"Then your mouth must be healthier than all of us put together," Quenton moaned. "Who cares about the news? It's boring!"

"It is not!" Rachel said indignantly. "It's important. It's informative. Oh, and I almost forgot! They're saying this Donny 'the Meatball' jail break is the biggest in a decade! The guy's ruthless. Did you know that he actually killed a man with a plastic spoon?"

"No!" Quenton leapt forward in his seat, his eyes bulging.

"But you wouldn't be interested in that," Rachel said curtly. "That's just boring news." She turned back to Anna. "There are all these rumors that the Meatball broke out of prison for a really big reason. He's got something new on his plate. Nobody's sure what he's up to yet, but the police are—"

"YOU SHUT YOUR TRAP! STOP TALKING ABOUT THAT RIGHT NOW!" Jacob stalked into the room, his eyes two furious slits. He pounded a fist on Rachel's desk and softly seethed, "My dad has people who can take care of you, Riley. So you better watch what you talk about from now on."

Jacob turned to the class, his voice rising in volume. "Hey, Riley, your mouth is bigger than the Holland Tunnel! It's no wonder your dad left." He smiled smugly. "If I had to live in a tiny apartment with you yapping all day long, I'd leave too."

Rachel's eyes flooded with tears. She grabbed her bag and fled the room.

Anna wandered down the hall looking for Rachel and thinking about stupid Jacob Pierce. Why did he just lose it like that? Why did he even care *what* Rachel talked about? And what was all of that junk that he was saying about his father? One thing was certain—Mr. Pierce was mixed up in something shady. And Anna couldn't help but wonder if it was Mr. Who related.

She shivered at that name and forced herself to think of more important things. This was her first chance to help someone—just like Ms. Sinclair had helped her—and Anna didn't want to blow it.

She found Rachel in the girl's bathroom; tears streaked her cheeks and her two blondish braids hung down the front of her blouse forlornly.

"Rach," Anna said softly, motioning for her to take a seat on the sink. "Want to talk about it?"

"What's there to talk about?" Rachel said, her voice shaking. "I have a big mouth!"

Anna handed Rachel a paper towel. "But do *you* think you have a big mouth?"

"I-I don't know." Rachel looked puzzled. "I just think that there are so many things going on in the world that are so important, and I guess I just want people to know what they are."

Anna nodded. "I can understand that. But let me ask

you something. Let's say there are two people—one person is jumping up and down, waving her hands and yelling. The other person is smiling quietly and raising her hand. Who would *you* want to listen to?"

Rachel thought for a moment and then nodded. "Yeah, I see your point. I come on a little strong."

"You gotta give people a choice, Rach. You don't have to cram their ears full of information, especially if they don't feel like hearing it. Maybe you could write it out or something. And whoever feels like it, will read it."

Rachel suddenly squealed with delight, jumping up from the sink. "That's it! That's it! I'm going to make a news bulletin board!"

"Cool." Anna grinned. "I mean you're already a reporter, Rachel. Why not make it official?"

"Anna! Anna!" Rachel shrieked, jumping up and down with excitement, her hair leaping to the very tops of the bathroom stalls. "Thank you! Thank you!"

Anna ducked so as not to get whacked by Rachel's braids.

"But if I'm a reporter, what are you?"

"Isn't that obvious?" Anna said with a smile.

"I'm the shrink."

.•.

Anna practically skipped down the hallway, a smile drawn across her face from ear to ear. It was a success! Already, she had helped someone. And it was all thanks to—

"Ms. Sinclair!" Anna picked up the pace when she saw

a familiar figure standing with one of the many police officers that still prowled the hallways. "Ms. Sinclair! It worked! Just like you—"

"Why won't you listen to me?!" Ms. Sinclair yelled at the police officer, her fists clenched into tight angry balls. "I know my sister! And she didn't go nuts without a reason! You need to do your job! You need to find the truth!!" She stifled a hiccupped sob.

"Ms. Sinclair," Anna breathed. "Are you OK?"

The guidance counselor wiped her puffy eyes with a tissue. "She's my older sister...Mrs. Summer."

Anna suddenly recalled Mrs. Summer leaving Ms. Sinclair's office yesterday—the curly hair and the large hazel eyes both women shared.

"Is there anything I can do?"

Ms. Sinclair steadied herself with a hand on Anna's shoulder. She managed one last desperate plea at the police officer's back as he shrugged and walked away. "Someone needs to find out what happened to her!" she cried after him. "S-Someone needs to find out—"

Too upset to continue, Ms. Sinclair disappeared into her room, shutting the door with a loud click. Anna stared at the closed door for a few moments. She could hear muffled crying inside. And then she reached her hand out, placing her palm against the smooth wood. "Don't worry," she said softly. "I will..."

There was only one thing the very large man wanted. During his four long years in prison he thought about this one thing the most, he dreamed about it at night, and, in a way, he broke out of the slammer because the prison cafeteria didn't serve them: chocolate cannolis.

As the large man entered the Grace Building, he hardly noticed how the outside of the famous skyscraper curved all the way down to the sidewalk like an enormous slide, and he paid no attention to the long line of customers waiting to get into the restaurant on the 50th floor. The large man just licked his lips, imagining the cream-filled pastry. If a chocolate cannoli were a woman, he would marry it.

"Hey," a small boy cried, standing at the front of the line, "no cutting!"

The large man picked the small boy up and, much to the dismay of his mother, hung him on a nearby coat peg. Then he clomped into the restaurant and took a seat at a linen-covered table by the window. He tapped his fingers impatiently, waiting for his company to arrive.

"I have an itchy rash on my foot."

The large man looked up to see a short, sweaty bald man dressed in brown tweed. He quickly muttered the correct code sentence back to the guy. "Yeah, would you like me to scratch it for you?"

The bald man sat down.

"I must do quick clearance check," he said in a thick Russian accent before disappearing beneath the table. When he resurfaced there was a large pink gob on his thumb. He whipped out a pair of microscopic glasses and examined it carefully. "No, it is not plastic explosives. It is just old bubble gum. This table is clear."

"So...business must really be booming, huh?" The large man laughed. "Get it? Booming? And you're a bomb-maker?"

The bald bomb-maker's left cheek twitched irritably. "What do you want?"

"My boss, Mr. Who, would like you to make him a bomb. Just in case something goes wrong."

The bomb-maker raised his eyebrows in shock. "Mr. Who, you say?" He clasped his hands together to hide their tremor. "No problem. I am not wanting any trouble. What size should bomb be?"

"An itty-bitty bomb. Small enough to take out a brick wall. But nothing else."

"When do you—" Suddenly the bald bomb-maker pulled a rubber band from his pocket. He shot it at a woman squatting by a nearby table with a camera, her husband and kids smiling over a birthday cake.

"OW!" the woman squeaked, dropping her camera. "My eye!"

The bald bomb-maker turned back to the large man. "I cannot have my picture taken."

"Yeah, me neither. I gotta lose a few pounds." The large man patted his gut. "But I've been having this craving for a couple years..." He eagerly flagged down a waiter. "Yeah, gimme a plate of chocolate cannolis."

"I'm sorry, sir. But we don't have cannolis here."

"What?!!" the large man bellowed.

"Please, sir," the waiter gulped. "We don't have chocolate cannolis."

"No cannolis?" Feeling his face grow as hot as a volcano, the large man pushed back his chair, ready to erupt. He reached over and lifted the waiter high in the air so his feet dangled down like a puppet's. Then he threw the man across the room where he landed beneath someone's table like a sack of potatoes. Customers screamed and huddled together.

Ignoring the terrified people, the large man marched across the dining room and disappeared into the kitchen only to reappear with a plate piled high with pastries—danishes, cookies, muffins, brownies and a few scones with blueberries.

"This will have to do, I guess," he mumbled to the bald bomb-maker, plopping back down in his seat. Then he proceeded to do what he liked best: *eat.*

Filed Under "D"

"Field trip! Yeah, field trip!"

"Yeah! Yeah! Field trip, dude!"

Quenton Cohen watched two kids high-five each other and turned to Anna, his face scrunched up in disbelief. "Give me a break. We're on a field trip at the *library*. You'd think we were at Six Flags or something."

Anna craned her neck, looking up into the massive reading room with its 52-foot-high ceilings, arching windows, enormous chandeliers and long oak tables with brass lamps. She had to admit, it was pretty cool.

"Quiet down! Quiet down!" Their tour guide called. "Shhhhh. What did I tell you children? We will be little mice today. Remember? Quiet as little mice."

"Great. I feel like I'm back in preschool," Quenton groaned. "I don't know if I can take much more of these animal-isms. Could someone please do something about that woman?"

Rachel squealed. "I know! Why don't you just give her some therapy, Anna?"

Quenton looked at Anna like she had hair sprouting from her nose. "Therapy?"

"Anna's a shrink!" Rachel said proudly. "A very good shrink. She gave me therapy, and now I'm going to be a reporter!"

Quenton crinkled up his nose.

"You'll see!" Rachel chided.

Anna just stared at her.

"What? I'm building you a client base!"

They were interrupted by the tour guide's animated voice. "You little puppies better be talking about the library! As I was saying the majority of the library's books are kept underground. There are over 88 miles of shelving, that extend out under Bryant Park to Sixth Avenue. We have a system of pneumatic tubes that help get a book up to the person who requested it as quickly as possible. Any questions, my little puppies?"

"If she calls us puppies one more time, I swear I'm going to lift my leg and go right on her!" Quenton grumbled.

"Gross!" Rachel chortled.

"How do the pneumatic tubes work?" asked a nasal voice.

Anna turned to see Simon Spektor holding his large box of tissues.

"Well, if you want to look at a book, you just fill out a call slip and hand it over to that clerk over there. The clerk rolls up your slip, puts it in a small canister, and sends the canister down the tubes to the underground bookshelves.

Someone down there finds your book and sends it up to the main reading room in a tiny elevator."

Quenton leaned over to Anna. "I can't believe you became a shrink and you didn't even tell me!"

"I'm sorry. It just sort of happened," Anna said. "Anyway, I was going to tell you at lunch."

"But I don't understand," Simon whined. "How do these tubes...the tube thingies work?"

Kids surrounding him looked at one another and sighed impatiently.

"Well, children," the Tour Guide explained in a slow voice. "When you push air into the tube, it sucks the little canister down. And when you reduce the air, the canister gets sucked backward again."

"Kind of like when you suck ginger ale up and down a straw?" Simon asked.

"Well, yes. I guess so," the tour guide replied, disdainfully eyeing Simon and the small pile of soiled tissues collecting at his feet. "Now I think it's time for you children to break for lunch—"

At the sound of the word "lunch," there was a whirlwind of feet, and everyone scattered.

"Finally!" said Quenton with an exasperated sigh. "Why was snotty Simon asking so many questions?"

"And none of that stuff he was asking was even news worthy," added Rachel. "Those tubes are so old they predate me!"

"Simon's not that bad, you guys." Anna snuck a look at the short boy bent over his tissue box. There was a large space surrounding him because no one wanted to stand too close. "He's actually kind of nice. I got to talk to him a little outside Principal Rollins's office yesterday."

"I hope you didn't get snot all over you!" said Rachel.

"Yeah, that boy should be in a hazmat suit," agreed Quenton.

"A what?"

"A hazardous-materials suit. You know, that get-up they wear when aliens send down a super-virus to wipe out humanity."

"You really have to stop watching so much cable, Quenton," Anna sighed, reaching for a library call slip and a pencil. "Um, guys, how should we fill this slip out? We're not looking for a specific book."

"This is so completely stupid! I can't believe we're actually doing this," Quenton grumbled.

"Quenton," scolded Anna, "Mrs. Summer was our art teacher!" *And also Ms. Sinclair's sister,* she thought sadly.

"Exactly!" chimed Rachel. "And we need to learn more about Mr. Who if we're going to find out what happened to her." She grabbed the pencil from Anna and began to scribble on the call slip. "All we have to put down is Mr. Who. Everyone knows who he is. I'm sure they have tons of books on him."

Anna watched Rachel, suddenly not sure this was the best way to find out information.

"Yes?" drawled the clerk behind the desk in a bored voice.

Rachel held out the slip and smiled perkily. "Hi there!

We didn't have an actual book to mark down, but we're looking for stuff on the criminal mastermind Mr. Who."

The clerk eyed them from behind a pair of thick-paned glasses. "Oh, him? He's filed under D. You know, for "DOESN'T EXIST!" Along with Batman, Wally the Were-wolf and the Easter Bunny." The clerk's desk phone rang. "You kids run along now. I have to take this call from Santa Claus."

RESTAURANT AT THE TOP
OF THE GRACE BUILDING

"PLACE BOTH OF YOUR HANDS IN THE AIR, MEATBALL!"

A cluster of police officers had quietly entered the restaurant, spread out along the perimeter of the dining room, and were now taking aim at the humongous man stuffing his face by the window.

The large man looked up from his chocolate cherry Danish, a mustache of powdered sugar dusting his upper lip. He slowly licked his fingers.

"I REPEAT, PUT YOUR HANDS IN THE AIR! WE HAVE YOU SURROUNDED!"

Now, the large man never liked to be interrupted during a meal. In fact, it made him very angry. So he rose from his seat, hands in the air, and panned the dining room for an escape route, but every door in the room was crawling with cops. There were only the massive windows overlooking Bryant Park behind him. And then a slow smile spread across the large man's face. He wiped his mouth with the back of his hand and glanced at the bald bomb-maker, who was pretending that he was sitting at the next table.

"Don't forget about the bomb thingy," the large man muttered, yanking a nearby tablecloth. "Mr. Who needs it soon."

Then, moving faster then a man of his size should, he lifted his table heaped with desserts and hurled it through the massive window with all his might. Glass crashed down in large, sharp triangles, and people screamed. The large man hopped onto the window ledge and stared down at the miniature traffic fifty floors below; the tablecloth he was holding blew in the wind like a large white flag...with food stains.

He whirled around one last time to glare at the dining-room staff.

"Your dessert stinks, suckers!!"

And then he jumped.

CHAPTER 9

Almost Mush

"I told you he didn't exist," muttered Quenton as they exited the Library and entered Bryant Park.

"Just because there are no library books on him doesn't mean he doesn't exist!" insisted Rachel pertinently. "Right, Anna?"

Anna didn't respond. She was beginning to agree with Quenton. Searching for Mr. Who was like camping out in the woods for a week and trying to spot Bigfoot. The guy wasn't real.

But Anna had no time to dwell on this because Quenton suddenly lifted a finger and pointed to something across the park. "Um, guys..."

Anna first noticed a clump of police cars and some policemen on horseback gathered outside the Grace Building, but as she looked higher...and then higher...and finally craned her head back to see what Quenton was pointing at, she gasped.

On the top floor, in a window with jagged chunks of broken glass poking out on all sides, stood a man. And then he jumped, using what looked like a large white tablecloth as a parachute.

"Please tell me that's Mary Poppins," squeaked Quenton.

They watched, mouths gaping open, as the man slid down the curved outside of the building like it was a giant slide.

"I can't look!" wailed Rachel, unable to pry her eyes away.

The man flew off the end of the building and in midair kicked a policeman off his horse before landing in the saddle himself with a loud THUMP! Whinnying, the horse took off at full gallop toward the park.

Anna, Quenton and Rachel just stood in the middle of the lawn, the rest of the class sprawled around them, watching as the man on the horse furiously galloped in their direction. Two policemen on horseback followed close behind, and sirens began to blare.

"Guys..." said Quenton, his voice an octave higher than normal. "It looks like he's coming right toward us. This is bad. Very bad. Like, late night Cinemax bad."

Alarmed, teachers rose from the grass and immediately started to gather the class together in one big clump. "Kids! Stand up!! Step back, kids!"

Anna watched, frozen, as the man on the horse got closer and closer. He's going to run us over, she thought, terrified. Kids began to shriek; a couple started crying, Anna tried to push her way out of the crowd she was trapped in. And then the horse's legs left the ground in a giant leap, sailing right over them. Anna squeezed her eyes shut tight and held her breath. The air seemed frozen, and then the horse landed with an earthshaking clomp on the other side of them, its hooves pounding loudly as it raced toward the other end of the park.

"Is anyone hurt?" screamed a teacher.

The two policemen reared their horses to a stop when they reached Anna and the rest of her class.

"What are you doing?" cried one policeman, a frustrated look on his face as he watched the large man gallop away. "He's getting away!"

"I'm not gonna jump over a bunch of kids! Are you out of your mind?" the other policeman barked.

"Who in the world was that?" Quenton breathed.

"I don't know," Anna replied, having gotten her breath back. "I didn't even see his face."

"We were almost mush!" Rachel cried, turning to Anna, her face as white as a ghost. "I mean, if the horse hadn't made it...mush."

"I think I peed my pants," moaned Quenton, closely examining the front of his jeans.

.◆.

Back at school, Anna couldn't stop her hands from shaking. Rumors trickled through the hallway that the man on horseback who almost mushed them was—

"Donny 'the Meatball' Fratelli," said Rachel, joining Anna by her locker. "Can you believe it? I'm telling you, Anna, strange stuff is happening. And I'm going to get to the bottom of it. Mr. Who is real! And for some reason he messed with our art teacher. Mrs. Summer losing her mind was not just one of those things, if you know what I mean. Someone—"

Rachel suddenly broke off and nudged Anna in the ribs. "Look!" she hissed.

Anna turned, rubbing her side, and saw someone in a black studded motorcycle jacket and black jeans: Clea Rodriguez. But Clea wasn't walking with her usual don't-mess-with-me swagger, nor was she wearing her headphones cranked to maximum volume. Rather, she was doing her best not to get noticed, edging down the hallway with her head down. When she reached the corner, she glanced around furtively and dodged toward the downstairs staircase.

"Come on!" hissed Rachel, taking Anna's arm.

They quietly followed Clea down the stairs and watched as she slipped beneath the yellow police tape and disappeared through the door of the art room.

Rachel turned to Anna, her eyebrows raised. "Why is *she* sneaking into the art room?"

Before Anna could answer, the final bell rang. Anna and Rachel traded mortified looks before scampering back upstairs and down the hallway. They slid to a stop right outside the math room, but the door was already closed.

"Remember what those cops told Rollins?" Rachel whispered. "They could have been talking about Ms. Musashi. I bet that stick of hers kills on contact."

Anna smiled weakly.

"Maybe you should give her some therapy?" Rachel suggested sincerely.

"I think her problems are a little too deep-rooted for that," Anna mumbled, silently turning the doorknob and entering the room as quietly as she could. She tiptoed toward her empty desk next to Quenton, and just as she was about to slide into her chair—

"Smudge!" a sharp voice rang out. "I'm glad you feel this class is a picnic in Gramercy Park! This is the second time this week you've been late, and the week has barely begun. Explain yourself."

Anna looked at a glowering Ms. Musashi, searching for anything to help her out of this nightmare. All of a sudden, Anna noticed that the tip of Ms. Musashi's long stick, the part she always clenched in her hand, was a deep pink today, matching her outfit. How had she never noticed this before? Maybe she had just been too afraid to look.

"Smudge, I'm waiting!"

"I-uh, I like your outfit today," Anna said, not believing it as the words tumbled out of her mouth. "It matches your-uh, your stick beautifully!"

If silence could be loud, that was what it sounded like. Nobody in the room moved, or even seemed to breathe. All eyes were on Anna.

"You may take a seat, Smudge," Ms. Musashi finally muttered through clenched teeth.

Math class seemed to pass as usual, but Anna noticed that Ms. Musashi was a little more patient and a little less tyrannical. Soon the bell rang, and everyone scrambled to the door.

"Smudge, could you come over here, please?"

Anna felt a huge lump in her throat. Maybe now she would find out what the stick was used for after all! She turned and made her way to the front of the room.

Ms. Musashi waited until the last kid had exited, and then she fixed her piercing eyes on Anna. Anna braced herself.

"So you think the pink looks OK?" Ms. Musashi asked, her voice hushed in case someone should be hiding beneath a desk or something.

"Oh, yeah," Anna said, surprised at the question.

"You don't think it's a little much? A teacher, teaching a rigorous subject like math, wearing pink?"

"No, not at all! It looks very nice with your dark hair."

Ms. Musashi, looking slightly pleased, reached up and ran a hand over her straight pageboy haircut.

"So...you think math is a rigorous subject?" Anna asked, shifting slightly on her feet.

"Oh, yes!" Ms. Musashi said forcibly. "It is a subject of laws that cannot be broken, a subject of numbers whose value always remains the same!" She cracked her stick against the desk as if to instill these rules.

"Well, sometimes when a subject is already so rigorous, it's...er...kind of scary when you teach it in such a rigorous fashion."

"Scary?" Ms. Musashi said, standing up to her full height so that she towered over Anna.

Anna quickly took a step back. "Yeah, and you don't learn as much when you're scared, you know?"

Ms. Musashi thought about this rather intensely for a moment. Then she nodded.

"Ms. Musashi, have you ever tried smiling while you gave a lesson?"

"*Smiling,*" Ms. Musashi repeated, stone-faced, as if Anna had just said a word in a strange foreign language. Then she abruptly turned back to the blackboard. "You may go."

Anna headed toward the door.

"And Smudge!"

She froze.

"I'll expect you on time tomorrow."

CHAPTER 10

Dinner

Anna picked fretfully at her crab cakes as she sat in the beautiful Pool Room of the Four Seasons restaurant. It was the first time she had shared a meal with her parents in almost two weeks. Dinner was almost finished, and they still hadn't acknowledged her presence.

"When will you find out if we won the government shipping contract?"

"Darling, I don't know. I still haven't heard back from them."

As the crème de la crème of New York society dug into their expensive dishes, Anna stared out the restaurant's floor-to-ceiling windows overlooking the skyscrapers on Fifty-Second Street, wishing she was someplace else...someplace like Ms. Sinclair's room.

"But if we land this job," Anna's mother was saying, "if the government uses one of our ships to transport this container for the army—and everything goes well—maybe they'll start to use more of our ships on a regular basis!"

"That would be ideal," agreed Anna's father.

"But I don't understand," Anna's mother continued, flustered. "It's been long enough for them to make a decision. Why haven't we heard anything back yet?"

Anna's heart began to beat like a sledgehammer.

"Well, there weren't any messages on my answering machine so I guess a decision hasn't yet been reached."

Anna dropped her fork. It thudded onto the carpet. She crawled under the table to fetch it and then sat there, half covered by the starched white tablecloth, not wanting to come back up.

"Anna dear, what are you doing down there?" Her mother called, finally noticing that she wasn't in her chair.

Anna just sat there holding the fork, thinking about the two blinking messages she had erased. Could one of them have been an important business call from the government?

"Anna, come back up here. We'll get you another fork."

Slowly, Anna pushed herself back up to her plush leather chair. "I don't need another fork," she said quietly. "I'm not really that hungry."

"So how was your day, pumpkin? Anything exciting happen?" her father asked absentmindedly as he flagged a waiter for more water.

Anna thought about the blackmail note and therapy; she remembered Mrs. Summer's crazy eyes as she ran around the hallway in a straightjacket and the loud clump of hooves as the man who jumped out of the Grace Building leaped over her class.

"It was just another normal day," she replied. Then

Anna took a deep breath and said, "Parents' Day is next Wednesday. Everyone's parents are going. Are you guys going to be there?"

Anna's parents looked at one another.

"Your father and I have a very important business trip—"

"Can't you postpone it?" Anna interrupted, looking down at the table because her eyes were beginning to sting. "Everyone's parents are going to be there..."

"Pumpkin, your mother and I will try our very hardest, but we can't promise you anything."

Anna just sat there, feeling like a deflated balloon.

"Can we ask for the check? I have homework to do." *Double the homework, actually,* Anna thought with a sinking feeling.

"That's my girl. Our studious daughter!" Anna's father said with a chuckle.

When they got home, Anna quickly said goodnight by the elevator door and trudged upstairs, dragging her backpack behind her like a set of iron shackles.

7 **Days Ago**

CHAPTER 11

The Drop

At 6 a.m. Anna's alarm rang...again...and again... and again—

"I'm up, I'm up, so be quiet already!" Anna blindly groped for the clock radio and attempted to push the snooze button one last time even though she knew she couldn't.

She had hardly gotten any sleep last night with all the extra blackmail homework she had to do, and now she had to wake up early to drop off the stupid extra homework at Grand Central Station before 7:00...or else.

On the subway platform Anna was listening to an opera-singing violinist when she noticed Simon Spektor slumped over his handheld video game, his large box of tissues sticking out of his jacket pocket.

"Simon! Hey, Simon!" The boy looked highly alarmed as Anna approached him. "Good morning."

There was a silence.

"Is there something you need?" Simon asked in his nasal voice.

"No. I just thought I'd wait with you."

"Why?" Simon glared at Anna suspiciously.

Anna shrugged. "No reason. So how are you feeling?"

Simon reached for a tissue and noisily blew his nose. "Not good. I have this really itchy rash. It started out as this aching feeling, and then it started itching. It might be a heat rash, but I think it might be Carbunculosis. I'm going to see Dr. Burg about it."

A couple people standing nearby glanced at Simon and then edged away, heading farther down the platform.

Anna peered closely at Simon's face. "I don't see a rash."

The tip of Simon's ears turned red. "It's, um, not on my face."

"Oh," Anna replied, but then she eyed the bundles of layers that Simon was wrapped in—he was dressed for an Arctic winter, and it wasn't even that cold out.

"If you have a heat rash, why are you wearing so many layers?"

"So I don't get pneumonia, since my immune system's down because of the rash."

"Oh." Stumped, Anna tried to think of something to say, something positive. "Well, that's fantastic, Simon!"

Simon threw Anna a strange look. "What is?"

"That—that you're going to the doctor! You'll go to the doctor and he'll fix you up, right?"

Simon squinted at Anna through his thick glasses. "I guess."

"And after that you'll feel great! Right?"

"Not really."

Anna's smile faded. "But why not? Just think—your rash

will get treated! You know, I really think your problem is that you dwell on things. After you stop itching, why on earth wouldn't you feel great?"

"Because I'll still be sick!" Simon replied impatiently, before fiercely blowing his nose into a tissue. "I'll still have postnasal drip, an ear infection, a sore throat and an itchy feeling on my tongue that makes me feel like I might have Leukoplakia. That's why! Do you know what that feels like? To be sick all the time?"

Anna opened her mouth but couldn't think of anything to say.

"I didn't think so."

The subway screeched to an ear-splitting stop, letting loose a hoard of people. Simon turned and disappeared into one of the cars. Anna felt herself get swept up into the crowd and soon she was squashed inside another car, feeling very much like a sardine, and then all was black as the subway careened through the underground tunnels of Manhattan.

"Do you know what it feels like to be sick all the time?" The words echoed in Anna's head again. No, she didn't know how it felt. It probably felt awful. Worse than awful. And instead of helping Simon, she had done nothing but act like a royal jerk.

Anna walked straight into Grand Central Station, ignoring the sky-high ceilings painted with stars and constellations, ignoring the surrounding little shops selling scarves and flowers. The enormous clock stood in the center of the room surrounded by a thick crowd of people, and east of it, against one of the far walls, stood the Currency Exchange Booth, empty. Anna took the crumpled note from her pocket.

You will leave this sheet of homework under the currency exchange booth, east of the clock in Grand Central Station.

Anna approached the booth, extra homework in hand. She hesitated a moment. But then she thought of her parents and the serious trouble she'd be in. Glancing around the crowded terminal, she searched for her blackmailer. Then she quietly placed the homework on the shelf, and edged away, forcing herself not to look back.

CHAPTER 12

The Witness

Anna walked through the large red doors of Bendox thinking dreadful thoughts. She had made her first awful "drop" at Grand Central Station, she had probably jeopardized her father's very important business deal, and she had done nothing but make poor sickly Simon feel even lousier than he did already. How was she ever going to be a good shrink when she just made people feel worse?

"I'm a bad-luck charm," Anna muttered. "I'm a bad joke with no punchline. Wherever I go, bad things find me." She clunked her forehead against her locker, and a small note fluttered down from the slots.

MEET ME IN THE ART ROOM.
COME ALONE

Anna stared at the note, a funny feeling tingling up her spine. Did her blackmailer want to meet face to face? But this note looked different. It was written in artful handwriting, almost like an invitation. But should she accept this invitation?

She looked around the empty school hallway; it was eerily quiet. She was the only one here. She glanced down at the note. Well, not the *only* one. Anna took a deep breath, and like a determined soldier ready to face a potential ambush, she braced herself and walked toward the stairwell.

.ė.

There was yellow police tape covering the art-room door. Anna glanced around to make sure no one was watching before ducking under the tape and quietly turning the doorknob.

The minute she stepped into the room, she wanted to leave. All of the walls were covered from top to bottom with the scribble of a crazy person—sentences wrapped around the walls, written in orange, green, purple, and whatever other color paint Mrs. Summer was able to get her hands on.

I saw the boogie man.
He's real.
I saw him and the man with the purple shoes.
He threatened to kill my students and
finger paint with their blood.
I know who WHO is.

Anna slowly spun around in place, reading the walls like they were four nonsense-filled letters. It must have taken Mrs. Summer hours to do this. Even though she was having some sort of nervous breakdown, their art teacher was obviously reaching out, desperately trying to tell them something. Something horrible.

There was a rustle from the corner of the room. Anna froze. Suddenly, the quiet seemed too quiet; the walls were too bright; why had she come here alone? Just as Anna was about to dodge toward the door and make a run for the stairs, just as she was about to leave this scary room and never come back—no matter how many notes she got in her locker—a figure stepped out from behind a tall canvas.

"You?" Anna's jaw nearly dropped to the floor. "You left me this note?"

"I hear you're a good person to talk to."

Todd Brecken-Bayer stood in the corner of the room, the number 13 on his soccer jersey the same color as his sky-blue eyes.

"I hear you're a shrink. So you can't repeat what someone tells you in secret, right?"

Anna nodded.

"Well, I know what happened to Mrs. Summer."

"What?" Anna blurted out, stunned. "How?"

Todd slowly looked around at the walls, his face filled with grief. "Because I was there."

Yes, Anna had often daydreamed about what it might be

like to have a conversation with Todd Brecken-Bayer...but never in the spooky art room that their crazy teacher had scribbled all over. They sat at the large rectangular table in the center of the room. Todd's face was white as a sheet, and he clenched his hands together as he spoke.

"I-I was down by the Seaport on Monday night, playing basketball. It was dark, so I couldn't see much. But I saw this big, scary guy knock on Mrs. Summer's door. And when she answered, he said that Mr. Who wanted to see her."

Anna's jaw nearly dropped to the floor. "Oh my god! He's real? He's really real?"

Todd nodded miserably.

"So what happened next?"

"Then the big guy dragged Mrs. Summer over to this dark car parked by the curb. I hid behind some garbage cans so they couldn't see me. But I heard Mrs. Summer crying and pleading with the guy. She was begging them to leave her alone, yelling that she could never sell her art shack and that she had already told them no! But you could hear it in her voice—she was scared to death."

"Her art shack?"

"Yeah. Mrs. Summer lives in this building by the pier that she calls her art shack. It's where she gives private lessons and has art shows. Sometimes she even has art shows for other artists. She's pretty generous that way—" Todd broke off, his head sagging into his hands.

"Todd," Anna said gently, "I know this is hard, but I need you to tell me what happened."

Todd took a shaky breath, his eyes filled with fear. "Then the big guy shoved her into the back of the car and shut the door. A few minutes later, a light went on in the back seat and Mrs. Summer just started screaming like a crazy person. I mean, she was always a little...but this was just..." Todd's voice choked.

"What was she screaming?" Anna asked, her heart pounding.

"She kept saying, 'You! It's you! Nooo! Nooo!' It was the most horrible thing I've ever heard. I-I haven't been able to sleep."

Anna exhaled. "That's terrible." She sat quietly for a minute, rolling this new information around in her head. Something still didn't sit right. She studied Todd out of the corner of her eye and noticed an odd sort of notebook peeking out from his backpack.

"Mrs. Summer was expecting someone that night, wasn't she? That's why she opened her door." Anna gestured to the notebook. "Why don't you tell me the *real* reason you were down by the Seaport, Todd?"

Surprised, Todd rose from his stool, but then he slumped back down again, defeated. He reached into his backpack and slowly pulled out the notebook. Only it wasn't a notebook, it was a large sketchpad. "I've been taking art lessons with Mrs. Summer on Monday nights... I didn't want anyone to know."

"Is that why you didn't call the police?"

"I did! I ran away and called right afterward. But the officer just laughed at me. He said that Mr. Who wasn't real, and if I felt like pulling a prank I should stick to the local pizza joint."

"What a jerk," Anna sighed, shaking her head. She looked at Todd's sketchpad and reached a hand out. "May I?"

Todd looked extremely reluctant, but he politely handed it over and stared down at the tabletop, embarrassed, as she began to flip pages. When Anna opened Todd's sketchpad, she nearly slid off her stool. Inside were sketches so good they looked real. Yes, Todd was the most popular kid in her grade. Yes, he was the best basketball player, along with being the best baseball player and soccer player and the last person standing in every dodgeball game...but art?

"I don't understand. Todd, these are absolutely amazing! You should be proud!"

"You sound like Mrs. Summer. She always encouraged me to show my art." Todd's blue eyes grew glassy. "Don't you see? This is all my fault! She saw Mr. Who and went crazy, and I didn't do anything to stop it!"

Without thinking, Anna reached across the table and took Todd's hand. "There was nothing you could have done. You would have just gotten yourself hurt, and that wouldn't have solved anything. It's not your fault, Todd."

Footsteps and voices filtered in from the outside hallway. It was almost time to go to first period. They sat there in silence for a few moments.

"Todd, I want you to know that your secret is safe with me. I won't tell anyone about your art lessons if you don't want me to. But this thing that you heard. It's big. Maybe too big for just the two of us. I'd like to bring in some people I know. And don't worry, they're super smart."

.•.

"**If a** chipmunk mated with a monkey, would it be called a munk-monk?" asked Quenton."

"Don't be ridiculous, Quenton!" said Rachel indignantly. "It would be called a chip-key."

"What if a hippopotamus got with a giraffe?"

"Oh, definitely a giraffamus," replied Rachel gravely.

"Um, guys," Anna snuck an embarrassed glance at Todd, who was starting to look a little worried. "Let's get back to the topic at hand."

"Right, right. So let me get this straight," grumbled Quenton. "The famous criminal mastermind Mr. Who is real. And not only does he exist, but he wants our old crazy art teacher's love shack—"

"Art shack," corrected Todd.

Anna gave Todd an encouraging look. She knew it must be have been hard for him to repeat the story again for Quenton and Rachel.

"Yeah, yeah, whatever," said Quenton, taking out a bag of homemade chocolate truffles and popping one into his mouth. "That's just bizarre. Why does Mr. Who want some dinky love shack?"

"Art shack, Quenton!" corrected Rachel.

"Yeah, yeah. I mean, what's so special about a dinky art shack?"

"I don't know," said Rachel, a mischievous smile creeping to her lips. "But we have forty minutes until the next period to find out."

CHAPTER 13

Men with Guns

"This is it. Right here," said Todd, stopping in front of a small two-story brick building. "This is where Mrs. Summer lives...er, lived."

Anna crinkled up her nose. "Yuck. It smells like fish."

"Hmm. I should make some fresh flounder tonight," mumbled Quenton.

"It smells like fish because we're right by the Seaport. See?" Rachel pointed to a cluster of multicolored ship masts peeking out from behind the building.

Anna couldn't help but think of her father. One of his ships was docked here...the one he had named after her. She wondered if it was the ship her father planned on using for his new job... if he won the contract. She quickly crossed her fingers, hoping she hadn't erased the wrong message.

"Well, there's absolutely nothing suspicious-looking about this place!" concluded Rachel, coming around from the back of the building.

"What about the inside?" Anna suggested.

Todd shook his head. "The whole downstairs is just full of art supplies, and then upstairs is where Mrs. Summer sleeps. There's really nothing out of the ordinary."

"This is a dead end. Let's go back to school and grab some lunch."

"It's chili. I saw someone carrying a bowl of it. It looks like boogers and beans—"

"HEY, GUYS! You're never going to believe this! Check this out!" shouted Quenton.

They hurried over to the decrepit brick building directly next to Mrs. Summer's; it was large and squat and looked like an old abandoned warehouse. Anna peered up at the arched doorway and was shocked to see the writing:

THE BENDOX SCHOOL

"This must have been where Bendox used to be when it was just a tiny all-boys boarding school!" exclaimed Rachel.

"Yeah, I remember hearing about that," nodded Quenton. "About twenty years ago, they decided to expand and moved uptown."

"It looks like this was the old gym," said Todd shaking his head. "I can't believe I never noticed this before!" He stepped back, surveying the two buildings. "Yeah, this is definitely an old gym. Then Mrs. Summer must live where the old dorms were."

They spread around the front of the building, trying to peer into the dirt-streaked windows. Without thinking,

Anna walked to the front door underneath the old archway and tugged on it...and it opened...and out stepped
two large guards as thick as tree trunks. They were
dressed in black military fatigues, each wore a headset,
and in their hands were huge machine guns. One of them
peered down at Anna. "You kids shouldn't be here. Run
along and play."

And they did. Anna, Quenton, Rachel and Todd ran as
fast as they could and didn't stop until they were inside a
subway car zooming back up to the Bendox School. The
new Bendox School. The one without armed guards.

.•.

"OK. Anyone want to tell me what G.I. Joe and his buddy
were doing in an old abandoned school gym?" Quenton
was leaning against a locker still slightly out of breath
from their sprint.

"They're guarding something," answered Todd.

There was a heavy silence.

"We have to find out what's in there," Rachel said quietly. "We have to find some way of getting inside."

"No duh, Rachel!" snorted Quenton. "But in case you
didn't notice, those meatheads had machine guns! How
are we going to get past them?"

Stumped, they slid down the front of their lockers and
sprawled out on the floor. Anna stared at her sneakers and
wondered what all of this had to do with Mrs. Summer.

.•.

Anna was getting books out of her locker for the next class when someone tapped her lightly on the shoulder. She turned to see Todd leaning against the neighboring locker, smiling. He was holding out a small package wrapped in paper.

"For me?" Anna asked in disbelief, taking the package and carefully unfolding the paper.

"I spent all morning working on them."

Anna sucked in a breath as she unveiled a thick pile of cards. Each one was cornflower blue, fading into a soft lavender at the corners. Artful writing was printed in the center.

Anna Smudge
PROFESSIONAL SHRINK

Do you feel alone?
Need someone to listen?
Someone to understand?

Call Anna for help. (212) 555-0174

"I hope you like them."

"Todd! These are...these are..." Anna shook her head, at a loss for words.

"Well, I wanted to thank you. If I hadn't talked to you this morning...well, I don't know what I would've done."

Anna looked down at her feet, feeling her cheeks turn pink. "I just listened."

"No, you did more. I was always embarrassed—always hiding my sketch pads and my art supplies. But you helped me feel proud of my art." Todd reached for Anna's hand. "Thank you."

He gave her hand a gentle squeeze and then strolled down the hallway and disappeared around the corner, leaving Anna with the cards pressed close to her heart.

CHAPTER 14

Free Advertisment

Math class was surprisingly pleasant that afternoon. Ms. Musashi wore an aquamarine outfit, and the tip of her stick was the same color. Anna noticed that she even attempted to smile a few times during the lesson. The result, however, was more disturbing than soothing, but by the end of the class her smiling attempts had improved greatly.

When the bell finally rang and all the kids filed out the door, Anna tentatively approached her math teacher's desk. "Um, Ms. Musashi," Anna shifted on her feet. "I just wanted to say, good class."

Anna watched, petrified, as Ms. Musashi's mouth quivered slightly before turning up into a haggard smile. "Thank you, Smudge," she mumbled.

"Oh, and I like the aquamarine too!"

At that, Ms. Musashi smiled once again, looking slightly happier this time.

"And if you ever need to talk, I'm a shrink—er therapist—and I'm always around to listen." Anna pulled out a thick pile of her new business cards, undoing the rubber band holding them together. Proudly, she handed one to Ms. Musashi. "So feel free to call any time." She started to put the rubber band back around the cards when—

"No! That is just unacceptable!" Ms. Musashi turned away to rummage through her briefcase, unlocking eight combination locks in the process. Anna watched fearfully, her mind racing. Why did she lock her briefcase with eight locks? What was Ms. Musashi mixed up in? Was she going to use her stick?

"This is more acceptable."

Ms. Musashi reached across the desk and handed a small leather case to Anna. It was covered with delicate engravings of flowers and trees in fascinating detail, and it seemed very old.

"It's beautiful!" Anna breathed.

"It was my mother's." Ms. Musashi said with a sad smile. "You can use it to hold your business cards. That rubber band just won't do."

Anna started to protest, "I couldn't possibly—"

"No. Take it. My mother always intended for me to give it to my own daughter, but I don't have any children. I have a young niece, but...I think she might be dead."

Anna opened her mouth to say something.

"But I'm happy. I have forty kids who I get to discipline—I mean teach everyday. Anyway, I do other work too."

Anna was about to ask what other work she was talking about when Ms. Musashi said sharply, "Take it." Then her features softened, and she said in a quiet voice, "It's been a long time since anyone has really *seen* me. Thank you."

Anna stood awkwardly in place, holding the case to her chest. She wanted to do something more to show how grateful she was, but she wasn't sure how Ms. Musashi would react if she tried giving her a hug. Rather, Anna slowly left the classroom, turning back one more time to see Ms. Musashi sitting at her desk under the harsh flores-cent light, peacefully grading papers.

At the end of the day, Anna waited for Quenton's dad, clutching the leather case Ms. Musashi had given her. She ran her finger across the smooth leather, admiring the del-icate flowers of its trim. She smiled, thinking of all the people she'd helped so far.

And then she saw Simon. He was slouching by the doors of the school, tissue box in one hand, his handheld video-game player in the other.

"Simon! Hey, Simon!"

He backed away as Anna approached. "I'm sick. I wouldn't come too close."

Anna stopped and took a deep breath. "Listen, I just wanted to apologize for how I acted on the subway plat—"

Suddenly, somebody pushed Anna. A sharp elbow jabbed into her back and the case was snatched out of her hand.

"Hey! Give that back!"

Jacob sauntered out toward the curb, examining the

leather case. He stuck his grimy fingers inside it, pulling out a slew of business cards. *"Call Anna for help,"* He cried in a mocking voice.

"Wow, Jacob, I didn't know you could read!" Quenton exclaimed as he strode through the large red doors. Rachel covered her mouth, trying to contain her laughter.

"You think you're so funny, Cohen, don't you?" Jacob snarled.

Anna clenched her fists together. Her back ached where Jacob had elbowed her. She tried to control her voice. "Give me back my case, Jacob."

"Ohhhh! *Give me back my case,*" Jacob mimicked in a high, piercing voice. "Make me!"

"Yeah, make him!" Roselyn joined her cousin, twirling her hair around a perfectly painted fingernail.

"I'll make him!" a voice said.

There was a silence. Anna turned to find Todd, his blue eyes resting on Jacob. Jacob's face drained in color, he looked nervous all of a sudden. Roselyn's finger froze mid-twirl.

"Fine," Jacob said. He stuffed his hand into the case, pulling out the remainder of the business cards, and tossed the case back at Anna. It hit her in the chest before falling to the concrete.

Anna bent down and quickly snatched it up. "Now give me back my business cards."

Just then, a loud honking filled the street as Mr. Pierce's cherry-red Viper pulled to the curb.

"My car's here," Jacob said, an evil glint in his eye. He

and Roselyn climbed into the Viper, the engine gunning. And then an unexpected figure stepped out in front of the car, clad head-to-toe in black leather, her hands on her hips—Clea Rodriguez stomped over to the driver's side door and she and Mr. Pierce began to argue, gesturing wildly. Clea smacked the door with a fist and the Viper pulled away, cutting off two other cars, and leaving behind a trail of angry drivers.

"What was that all about?" said Quenton.

"Yeah, how in the world does Clea know Mr. Pierce?" asked Rachel.

"They sure were going at it," remarked Todd.

Anna just stood there in disbelief, Ms. Musashi's empty case in her hands.

"Don't worry, Anna." Todd put a hand on her arm. "I'll make you new cards—"

"HEY, SLUDGE!"

There were shouts, and a flash of cherry zoomed around the block again.

"YO, SLUDGE!" yelled Jacob, holding his hand out. "You want your cards back? Well, you're gonna have to get all the bums in New York City to help you pick them up!" He opened up his hand, and a cluster of Anna's business cards blew out into the street. Anna watched, horrified, as the car sped up the block and around the corner, cards spewing from it, blowing every which way.

Anna shook her head. It was just too much.

"What a waste of a nice car," Quenton muttered, gazing down the empty street after the Viper.

"Quenton!" Rachel scolded. "Anna's business cards will be all over the city now!"

Quenton shrugged and turned to Anna. "It's free advertising. That's how you've got to look at it. Hey, maybe my dad should do something like that for the store. I mean, you never know who's going to see it."

The large man stood on top of the Brooklyn Bridge and stared down at the dark ripples of the East River, one hundred and thirty-five feet below. He had come to this place to remember the past; the large man had thrown quite a number of people from the top of this bridge. But lately, his heart just wasn't in it anymore. Being a criminal wasn't like it used to be. It wasn't fun. The long chase through Bryant Park had left him exhausted, and ever since he climbed down from that horse, he had been walking kind of funny.

The large man felt the buzz of his cell phone. "Yeah?" he said, clicking the phone open with a large hand.

"Mr. Fratelli," said a voice as smooth as silk. "What did Mr. Smudge say about retracting his bid for the government job?"

The large man gulped. "I haven't talked to Mr. Smudge yet."

"WHAT?!"

"Well, I left that message on his answering machine. Just like I told ya, boss."

"And he hasn't returned your call?"

"Nope."

"How dare he!" the voice growled. "Time is ticking away. Can you hear it Mr. Fratelli? Tick, tick, tick. The government will choose a shipping company soon, and I need them to choose *my* company. I need them to use *my* ship to transport the cargo so that I can steal back what's mine without them realizing it's getting away."

"That's pretty smart, boss."

"Mr. Fratelli," crooned the voice, "I believe it's time for Mr. Smudge to meet his expiration date."

The large man scratched his head. He was confused. Expiration date? Could people go bad just like milk and cheese did if you kept them in the fridge too long? The large man wrinkled his nose at the thought. He had eaten sour cheese once. It was nasty.

"Um, I don't get it, boss, sir. What do you mean by expiration—"

"IDIOT!" roared the voice impatiently. "Kill Mr. Smudge! You have one week! Do the hit...or I'll put a hit on YOU!"

"Yes, Mr. Who," the large man replied through gritted teeth.

Then the line went dead.

The large man was clenching his cell phone so tightly, it had cracked down the center. He chucked it over the side of the bridge and watched it splash into the cold water below. No, it wasn't like it used to be, being a criminal. Maybe after this hit he needed a career change? The large man reached up to touch his newly bleached hair. He had just bought a box of Clairol at the cosmetics store—platinum blonde, a color that he felt best suited his skintone—and had done the job himself. Maybe he could go into the beauty profession?

Just then, a large gust of wind blew a pile of dirt and debris across the bridge and over the large man's feet. He bent over to dust off his suede shoes when he noticed a small card sticking to his left foot. Part of the writing on the card was smudged with dirt, but he could make out some of it. "Yes," thought the large man, nodding, "I need some help." And he picked up the card.

CHAPTER 15

A Sleepless Night

Anna was startled awake by the ringing of the telephone. She had fallen asleep while working on all of her extra homework, the blackmail note lying on the bed next to her as a reminder of what would happen if she didn't finish.

"Hello?" she answered groggily.

"Is this Anna Smudge?" asked an unfamiliar voice.

"Yes," Anna replied.

"Because I'm babysitting..."

Who on earth was this? It sure didn't sound like any of her friends.

"...and, well, I accidentally let the cat out of the townhouse," the voice continued. "And now its climbed up a tree in Central Park. The owners will be home soon, and I can't get the cat down! What should I do?"

"Um, I'm not really sure."

"Well what good are you, then?" snapped the voice. "Free help, my butt!"

Puzzled, Anna hung up the phone, and that's when she realized it. Stupid Jacob Pierce! Because of *him*, every nut in New York City had probably picked up one of her business cards. Now all of Manhattan would be calling!

The phone sounded again. Anna scrambled to pick it up so her parents wouldn't hear.

"The sink in my bathroom is leaking!" a deep voice jumped right in. "I'm not sure if it's the faucet or the pipes or what. Should I go out and buy a wrench, or should I just try and superglue it?"

"I don't know!" Anna replied, annoyed. "I'm not a plumber, I'm a *shrink!* You know—a therapist?"

"Oh," said the deep voice. "Well, I might need some therapy if I can't get this darn sink fixed. Maybe I'll be in touch later. Thanks."

Anna hung up and took a few long, deep breaths when... the phone rang. "Hello," she answered glibly. "And I'm a therapist, not a plumber!"

There was a silence.

"Um, that's good. 'Cause I was calling to get some therapy and not, um, get my toilet fixed. You see, I'm a little messed-up right now, and I wanna make an appointment with Anna...Anna something...I can't really make out the rest of the name, 'cause I think there's bird doo on the card."

Anna sat up straight. "I'm so sorry," she said, trying to sound professional. "This is Anna. I've been getting, er, crank calls. Kids, you know?"

"Yeah, I hate kids."

"So if you'd like to schedule an appointment, I'd be happy to meet with you tomorrow. What's your name?"

There was a silence at the other end of the line.

"Hello?" Anna said, afraid that they might have gotten disconnected.

"My name...my name is Folgers."

"Oh, like the coffee?"

There was another silence.

"So what time is good for you, Mr. Folgers?"

"Anytime. I'm free as a bird!" A nervous laugh sounded into the receiver. "Where's your office?

"My office," Anna repeated. "Um, well I'm, uh, currently getting a new space." Anna grabbed a notebook. "So if I could get your number and give you a call back—"

"No. I'll call you!"

Then there was a dial tone. Mr. Folgers had hung up.

Anna slumped back onto her pillow. *Her office.* Where was she going to find an office? She definitely couldn't use her bedroom—it wasn't professional. And there was no way she could use any room of the apartment without her parents finding out.

The phone rang again.

"Hi. Can you help me win the lottery?"

Anna sighed. It was going to be a long night.

Anna had to take the phone off the receiver because it just would not stop ringing. Then she snuck downstairs and hopped in the elevator.

"Why, Miss Anna, what are you doing up at this late hour?" Percy, the doorman, exclaimed.

"Let's just say I'm more popular than I've ever been," Anna said wryly. "You see, I've recently become a professional shrink. I've already gotten a few calls—well, a lot of calls—but I just don't have anywhere for these people to go to conduct a session. I need an office."

Percy's face brightened and he strode toward the back of the lobby, motioning Anna to follow. "Some say it is quite lucky to have a room without windows. If you do not see the sunrise, then you are forced to create your own!" And with that, Percy swung a door open. Inside was an empty but nice-sized room with no windows.

"It used to be an old storage closet. It'll definitely need some fixing up, but don't you bat an eye about that. Polished Percy can take care of it while you're at school. There's nothing like a nice Irish touch to heal the tormented!" Percy said with a wink. "Besides, I like your office being down here—that way I can keep my eye on you."

"Thank you so much, Percy! I knew I could count on you!"

Percy took Anna's hand in his large rough one and gave it a shake. "May the roof above us never fall in, and may the friends gathered below it never fall out!"

"Percy," Anna said thoughtfully. "You know every Irish superstition, toast, remedy, curse, everything! Why don't you write a book?"

"A book?" Percy repeated.

"Yes, share your knowledge with the world!"

"Yes, I could, couldn't I?" Percy said, his green eyes twinkling mischievously.

6 Days Ago

The Naked Seaweed Man

Anna was exhausted. A sleepless night of end-less phone calls and homework had taken its toll, and she had barely made it out of bed in time to drop her extra homework off at Grand Central. She honestly didn't know how much more of this blackmail stuff she could take.

Anna surfaced from the subway and walked toward Bendox.

"Well, hello, Mr. Who! It's sooo nice of you to call!"

Anna's heart jumped, and she quickly spun around. But it was just Quenton holding a giant banana to his ear, pretending it was a cell phone.

"I was wondering when you were going to notice me. I've been following you for almost a block! Way to be aware of Stranger Danger." Quenton unpeeled the banana and took a bite.

Anna sighed heavily. "Yeah, well, I'm ex-hausted. I didn't get one wink of sleep last night. I think every freak in the city must have picked up one of my new—"

Anna broke off as they rounded the corner.

There was a huge crowd out in front of the school—
hordes of kids and even a few teachers eagerly huddled
together, and a bunch of news vans were parked on the
curb. Was someone famous here?

"There she is!"

A pretty woman stepped out from the crowd, her hair
so blonde it was almost white. She smiled, revealing two
rows of perfect shiny teeth. "Anna Smudge, I'm Lora Bora
with the Channel Five News! We'd like to interview you
for our prime time edition."

"Me?" Anna finally managed. "Why?"

"Why, Miss Smudge, you're an overnight sensation!"

"I am?" Anna felt the color drain from her face.

"Let's start!" Lora said, clasping a microphone and
turning toward the camera. "Good morning, New York!
I'm here with the youngest shrink in the city. The very
neurotic might already know her name: Anna Smudge."

The camera swung around, nearly blinding Anna with
its bright light.

"So, Anna, our viewers would like to know, what do
you do to unwind at the end of a busy day?"

"Er...my homework."

Lora nodded at the camera knowingly. "Like most of us
in the city, a workaholic. Tell me, Anna, is there anything
you'd like to say to your many fans?"

"My fans?" Anna broke off as she looked down the
block. An army of people were collecting around the school,
throngs of all sorts of New Yorkers, every one of them clasping one of her business cards.

"YO, ANNA!" cried a chubby man wearing a frilly nightgown, an Egyptian crown and heavy black eye make-up. "I just found out that in a past life I was Cleopatra. It is not for me that I seek therapy, it is for the troubled woman I once was."

"Greetings, Earthling Anna!" chimed a man wearing a silver jumpsuit. He was carrying a blowup doll and a lobster. "I am from the planet Uugh, and this is my wife Uugly, and our pet Uuglier. Can you help us get home?"

Quenton elbowed someone in a papaya costume out of the way. "It's like a regular fruit salad out here!" He yanked Anna's arm, pulling her through the growing swarm. Anna smiled weakly at a businesswoman arguing with her hand puppet and side-stepped past an old lady carrying a dozen bags of used dental floss. "Never neglect your gums!" she called after Anna with a toothless grin.

"YO, ANNA," cried Cleopatra. "I brought my buddy from the docks, Dr. LeGrande. Can you help him out?"

Suddenly, a hush spread. The crowd parted, and Dr. Le-Grande stepped forward. He had one milky-white eye that glistened like a marble, he was dripping wet, completely naked, and draped with seaweed. He twirled around and around, slinging saltwater everywhere, and then stopped abruptly in front of Anna, dead serious.

> *I made a box. A box I made.*
> *And for this special box he paid.*
> *No name has he. He has no name.*
> *To Mr. Who it's all a game.*

He pushed me out. He made me drown.
Survive I did. I swam somehow.
He'll kill us all! He'll make us drop!
Unless you find a way to stop.... um, him.

Quenton elbowed Anna out of the way, his jaw dropping open as he stared at the naked seaweed man. "UNCLE BRIAN?!"

Quenton sat morosely on a bench in the school foyer. He looked up at Anna and Rachel and sadly shook his head.

"I haven't seen Uncle Brian since—since I was about seven! My mom stopped speaking to him. She told us he was involved with a rotten crowd. That's how he hurt his eye."

Anna thought of Quenton's mom and how proper she was. It made sense that she wouldn't want her children hanging around her brother, especially if he was involved with—

"Mr. Who!" Rachel exclaimed. "Quenton, why didn't you tell us your uncle is involved with Mr. Who?"

"How was I supposed to know?" snapped Quenton. He buried his face in his hands. "Like I'm not traumatized enough seeing my uncle butt-naked."

"Quenton, what did your uncle do? He was talking about some sort of box that he made?"

"He was a scientist—an engineer, I think. My mom says

he makes these small sealed greenhouse thingies for growing special plants. They're completely airtight."

Anna shook her head, utterly confused. "But what could
he be doing for Mr. Who?"

"Well, you heard him," replied Quenton sheepishly. "He
must have built Mr. Who some kind of box. And then Mr.
Who tried to drown him or something. I don't know!"
Quenton stood up, exasperated. "The guy speaks in
rhymes! How on earth am I supposed to understand him?
And is it me, or is everyone in this city crazy?"

Just then, a police officer stuck his head through the
door. "Hey, kid. The ambulance is here."

"I guess I have to go wait with Uncle Brian until my
mom gets here."

Rachel followed him to the door. "I'll go with you,
Quenton."

"I hope they made him put some pants on. Those bar-
nacles don't cover up much."

Rachel turned to Anna before exiting. "It's probably
best if you wait here. That crowd doesn't look like it's leaving anytime soon. See you later."

As they opened the door, the crowd outside roared for
Anna, and then the door clicked shut leaving the school
foyer in silence. Most of the kids had gone outside to watch
all the commotion; there were just a few bent over their
notebooks, scrambling to finish their homework before first
period. And that's when Anna spotted Amy Lerner. She
was standing alone in the corner, quietly looking down at

her feet. Anna hesitated a moment and then made her way over to the shy girl.

"Hi, Amy."

Amy looked up, a startled expression on her face.

"Mind if I wait with you?"

Amy looked as if she was going to pass out from shock but slowly shook her head.

"So, what do you think about that crowd, huh?"

"They scare me," Amy said timidly.

"Yeah, me too," agreed Anna. "Not that I'm complaining or anything. I mean this is what I want to do. Be a shrink. But I'm a little nervous though."

"Why?"

"Well, I have my first official therapy session after school today! I mean, my first session with a total stranger in my new office space, and—well, I just hope everything goes OK. My doorman, Percy, and I fixed up the room. It's a little more green than I wanted, but Percy insisted because, after all, green is lucky, and it is the color of Ireland."

"Is he really from Ireland?" Amy's eyes were opened wide with interest.

"Yup, he's got an accent and everything. And he has all these cool Irish sayings like…" Anna rolled up her sleeves to prepare for her Percy impression. Then she said in a thick Irish brogue, "Just remember, Miss Anna, may the Irish hills caress you. May her lakes and rivers bless you. May the luck of the Irish enfold you. May the blessings of Saint Patrick behold you!" She finished with a deep bow.

Amy burst into laughter. Then Anna started to giggle. Soon they were laughing so hard they were holding their sides in pain and gasping for air like two fishes out of their bowl.

"You should come over and meet him one day."

"OK" Amy said with a grin. But then the smile wilted from her face. "Oh, actually I can't."

"Why not?"

"Roselyn wouldn't like it."

"So? Who cares what Roselyn likes? She sure doesn't like me!" Anna chuckled. Amy remained silent.

"Amy, you're really fun! You should give everybody a chance to find that out."

"You think I'm fun?"

"Definitely. Do you even *like* Roselyn?"

Amy hesitated and looked around slowly. Then she turned to Anna and said, "I guess I don't like the way she treats people. But she's my only friend. She says that if she wasn't my friend, I wouldn't have any."

"Do you think a real friend would say that to you?"

Amy didn't reply.

The Hershey Handshake

Gym class.

Those two words were about as appealing as "chicken liver" or "Brussels sprouts." As Anna entered the gym, she tried to ignore the whispers and stares of her classmates. It was as if overnight, everyone in school suddenly knew who she was. Anna lined up against the wall next to Quenton as Ms. McGee took attendance.

"How are you doing?" she whispered.

"OK," Quenton replied. "I think I'm going to be skipping the sushi and anything else seaweed-related for a while. But other than that, I'm OK."

Just then, Simon Spektor wandered into the gym, tissue box in hand.

"Hi, Simon," Anna called as he shuffled by. "How are you feeling?"

"Horrible. I'm all congested, and I'm pretty sure I have ischemic cholitis, which is giving me horrible abdominal pains that make me want to vomit all the time, and my fibromyalgia is acting up, so it hurts to walk," replied the nasal voice. "I'm seeing Dr. Rabble about it this afternoon."

"Oh...well. Is there anything I can do?"

"No, I'll just suffer. I'm used to not being able to breathe through my nose at night. Thanks." Simon shuffled away while blowing his nose like a loud horn. Anna watched him go, feeling helpless. She looked at Quenton, who whistled and spun his finger around his temple.

"Stop, Quenton. I feel bad for him. He's got such poor health."

"No, he doesn't." Quenton rolled his eyes toward the ceiling. "It's all in his head. That guy's as crazy as a fruit fly. That guy's crazier than my crazy uncle."

"Oh, by the way," he added nonchalantly, "I didn't get a chance to tell you this morning, but I think I know how we can get past those guards with the machine guns."

Anna's breath caught in her throat. "How?"

"Well, remember that time when I was cooking a carrot stew in the teachers' lounge, and it bubbled over and got all over the floor? Well, while Rollins was chewing my head off, I remember staring at these old framed diagrams on the wall above his desk. Man, did I stare at them awhile!"

Quenton lowered his voice.

"Well, I think those diagrams might have been blueprints of the old Bendox School. If we could get a good look at them, they might show us another way in."

"That's the best idea you've had in ten and a half years!"

Anna and Quenton looked up to see Rachel smiling widely. She slumped down against the wall next to them. "But how do you plan on getting a look at those blueprints again if they're *inside* Principal Rollins's office?"

"Well, someone's going to have to get sent to Rollins's office on purpose." Quenton looked at Anna.

"No! No way!"

"Anna, it makes the most sense. You're the only one of us who already has a real juvie record. And we *have* to find out what's inside that old gym! It's connected to Mrs. Summer!"

Anna glared at Quenton and Rachel. "I am *not* going to get sent to Mr. Rollins's office on purpose. I'm already in enough trouble as it is, thank you very much!"

"Just bite someone else, Anna."

"I told you guys! I didn't—"

Ms. McGee blasted her whistle to silence the class. "OK, we have a choice today. We can either play dodgeball up on the roof again or we can stay in the gym and play Red Rover."

Immediately, Roselyn's hand shot up.

"Yes, Roselyn?"

"I would like to request that we stay in the gym because I have on new JoJo gym shorts, and I *can't* get them dirty! And Amy can't get hers dirty either, right Amy?"

All the color drained out of Amy's face. She quickly glanced at Anna and then looked away, nodding.

"OK, Red Rover it is. Split into two groups. The dividing line is here." Ms. McGee walked over to where Quenton and Anna stood and placed her hand between them. Slowly, they parted and headed over to opposite teams.

"I'm watching you, Smudge," Ms. McGee called. "Don't think I haven't heard about your little shenanigans."

Anna gritted her teeth and joined her team, who were already lined up holding hands. She walked over to the very end of the line, only to find…Jacob Pierce.

"Just grab my hand, Smudge," Jacob said with an evil grin.

Anna hesitated and looked back at Ms. McGee who was choosing a caller for the other team.

Jacob held out his hand. "C'mon, Smudge! *I* don't bite. That's what *you* do, remember?"

Ms. McGee turned and began walking toward their line to choose a caller. She would see that Anna wasn't holding hands with the next person in line like she was supposed to. Anna braced herself and grabbed Jacob's hand, and that's when she felt it—something warm and gooey. Anna tried to pull her hand away, but Jacob had it in a fierce clench, and then she looked down. There was a brown mushy substance oozing through her fingers.

"By the way, I forgot to wash my hands after I went to the little boy's room!" Jacob snickered. Then, before she could do anything, he let out a blood-curdling scream, snatching his hand back with fake disgust.

"Eeew! Help! Somebody! Smudge fudged on her hand and wiped it on me!" Jacob quickly wiped a little of the brown stuff onto his face. "Somebody get it off! Didn't your mommy teach you to wipe yourself, Smudge?"

CHAPTER 17

Ms. McGee ran over, a look of horror on her face. "What's going on here?"

"Anna told me that she didn't wipe herself in the bathroom, and—and she wiped it on me!" Jacob shrieked, his face contorting into a perfect expression of distress. "Get it off! Get it off!"

Ms. McGee looked beside herself. "Go to the locker room, Jacob, and get in the shower! And *you!*" She turned to a bewildered Anna. "I have no words! Just go! Just..." and without being able to even complete her sentence, an extremely red-faced Ms. McGee pointed toward the door. She didn't even have to say where to go. Anna already knew.

As she crossed the gymnasium, Anna spotted Rachel smiling excitedly and giving her the thumbs up. But where was Quenton? *Well, it looks like someone's getting sent to Rollins's office after all,* thought Anna. *And I didn't even have to bite anyone.*

Anna stared up at Thaddeus T. Rollins's perfectly polished wooden door, her brain working a million miles a minute. How in the world was she going to get to those blueprints of the old Bendox School if Principal Rollins was sitting right in front of them? Well, she'd have to figure out some way, quick. She raised a fist and was about to knock when—

The fire alarm began to ring. There was a loud bang as the doors to the teachers' lounge across the hall slammed open and a thick cloud of smoke escaped, pouring down the hallway like a fog. Through the gray plumes, Anna could make out a teacher holding a familiar figure by his ear.

"I told you—this is *supposed* to be on fire! Otherwise the presentation of the dish is ruined!" Quenton was wearing an apron. In one hand he clutched a large spatula and in the other—a frying pan filled with bright-orange flickering flames.

"Put those flames out this instant!" demanded the teacher, giving Quenton's ear another tug.

"WHAT IS THE MEANING OF THIS?! WHAT IS THIS ABOMINABLE RUCKUS?!" Principal Rollins stuck his neatly combed head out of his office, his brow furrowed, his eyes popping.

"Thaddeus," snapped the teacher. "This student was lighting things on fire in the teachers' lounge!"

"I was just making that banana flambée you like so much, Mr. Rollins."

Principal Rollins's eyes lit up. "Oh? Are you making it with honey?" He stepped out from his office and walked right by Anna, hardly even noticing she was there. "I do like it when you make it with honey." As the principal disappeared into the smoke-filled teachers' lounge, Quenton quickly winked at Anna before turning to follow him.

Anna shoved her foot into the doorway, catching Mr. Rollins's door before it closed, and stepped into his office.

The entire room was made of meticulously polished wood, and above the wooden desk, covering the wood-paneled wall, were tons of neatly framed pictures. There were paintings of the school, old black-and-white photographs of students from the 1920s, a picture of Mr. Rollins holding a very large fish, framed blueprints of the current Bendox School. And, finally, hanging right beneath a large wooden paddle with the engraving *Education takes discipline!*—blueprints of the old Bendox.

Anna closely examined the fading diagrams underneath the glass. The building to the left was the old dormitory where Mrs. Summer lived, and directly alongside it was the old gym with the two armed guards. Anna peered closer at the old gym, trying to get her bearings. There was that fire escape she had remembered seeing, but that was an obvious way in, and there could be more armed men guarding that opening. She examined a small room toward the back of the old gym, which must have been the locker room, and noticed a little rectangular thing on the back wall. It looked like a tiny window.

Suddenly, footsteps and voices sounded outside the door. Anna scrambled for her camera phone and began to furiously snap pictures of the blueprints.

"Well, gentlemen, I'm afraid that was just a false alarm." The doorknob turned, and Anna quickly ducked beneath the large wooden desk and held her breath. "There's no fire," explained Principal Rollins to a handful of firemen. Anna could see their large fireproof boots through the opening at the bottom of the desk. "But please come in and sit down while I make an announcement on the intercom."

A rising panic took hold of Anna as two perfectly polished shoes started toward her. And then a familiar voice sounded from the doorway.

"Hey, guys, I have warm chocolate hazelnut cookies fresh from the oven! Tell me what you think?"

The polished shoes halted right in front of Anna and then slowly started back toward the door. "Oh, I think we have time for one cookie...or maybe two..."

The door clicked shut. Anna waited a few seconds and then left the room running.

The Man with the Purple Shoes

Anna passed her camera phone around so everyone could get a look at the blueprints. She was pretty sure that small opening in back of the gym would be their best way inside, but everyone wanted to be extra thorough—after all, they were dealing with men with machine guns.

She was on her way to last period when she spotted Clea Rodriguez sneaking around again. The final bell rang. Anna hesitated a moment, feeling torn, and then quietly followed Clea down the stairs toward the art room.

"You following me?"

Anna froze...and then slowly turned to see Clea leaning against a wall, smirking. She wore a black T-shirt with a giant fist on it, black sweatpants with a design of skulls, and large black combat boots.

"Yo, I asked you a question, shrink girl!"

"Um..."

Suddenly, Clea broke out into a huge grin. She clapped Anna affectionately on the back.

"It's OK, you're cool. After all, you bit the turd!"

"Well, actually, I didn't really—"

"And any enemy of the Pierces is a friend of mine," continued Clea. "So I'm going to do something for you. I'm going to put together a little something that will prove Jacob gave you the Hershey Handshake."

Anna cringed. "The Hershey Handshake!" she repeated, feeling her cheeks grow hot. "You mean there's actually a name for that—that disgusting—"

"Relax, it was just a melted piece of chocolate. I saw him pull it out of his sock before class. I got it all right here." Clea lifted the camera she always wore around her neck on a studded strap. "I'll make some blow-up shots for you this afternoon. I've got a place I can print them at." Clea gestured toward the door covered with yellow police tape.

Anna looked at Clea and then at her camera, suddenly realizing she had been sneaking into the art room to print her photos. "Um, thanks. But I don't understand. What do you have against Jacob?"

"He's obnoxious, and someone should teach him a lesson. Also, his dad's a big sleazy music producer. Mr. Pierce and I aren't very close, in case you haven't noticed. He really screwed over my dad."

"Your dad?"

"Yeah, Rage Rodriguez."

"Your dad is Rage Rodriguez?!" Anna exclaimed, nearly falling over. Rage Rodriguez was the lead singer of Blood & Rage, one of the most famous heavy-metal bands of all time. Anna owned their greatest hits album *All the Rage* and liked to listen to it while she did homework. "That is so cool!"

"My dad's working on his next album right now. I've been taking nonstop shots of the band so hopefully he'll want to use one for the album cover."

"Can I see?"

"Sure." Clea turned on the digital display and handed Anna her camera. Anna sifted through shots of people wearing lots of black leather and looking very angry while eating hoagies. She couldn't imagine having a rock star in the family. Suddenly, she gasped as she came to the last few pictures. "The man with the purple shoes!" she breathed.

"What was that?" said Clea.

Anna looked up from the camera, her heart pounding. "Clea, who is this person in these last few shots?"

"Oh, him? That's the guy Mr. Pierce sent to threaten my dad into signing with his label. He was this big deal hitman, Donny 'the Meatball' Fratelli. I was hiding behind the sofa when I took those, so I only got the guy's feet."

Anna gulped.

"You OK?" Clea said, throwing her a strange look.

Anna just nodded, unable to tear her eyes away from the humongous pair of suede shoes standing on a big furry rug. They were beautifully made, shockingly large and vividly purple.

"I know who the man with the purple shoes is!"

"That's great, Anna. I know a girl with yellow polka-dotted underwear. We should introduce them." Quenton pushed open the large red doors and stepped outside. Anna followed him.

"Quenton, don't you remember? Mrs. Summer talked about the Boogeyman and the man with the purple shoes. We know the Boogeyman was a reference to Mr. Who... but who is this man with the purple shoes?"

Quenton stopped in his tracks. "You know who he is?"

"That's what I've been trying to tell you! He's that escaped convict that nearly mushed us on horseback the other day—"

"Donny 'the Meatball' Fratelli?" Quenton said a little too loudly.

"Shhh!" Anna glanced around. The sidewalk was crowded with kids talking and exchanging text messages before leaving for the day.

"This is not good, Anna. That guy kills people with plastic spoons. I mean, spoons! They give those utensils to babies!"

"I know," Anna sighed. "And you want to hear something even more shady? Donny 'the Meatball' has done work for Mr. Pierce."

"I knew it! I knew Jacob's dad was bad news. That's why Jacob freaked out on Rachel that day when she was talking about Donny. He didn't want it to get out that his dad had hired the Meatball. It would be a major family scandal."

"So, Donny has done work for Mr. Pierce. But Donny

also works for Mr. Who," Anna said slowly. She looked up at Quenton, her eyes wide. "Do you think Mr. Pierce could *be* Mr. Who?"

Quenton was quiet for a long moment but then he looked directly at Anna. "If he is, you'd better go make BFF with Jacob Pierce right now."

CHAPTER 19

Chocolate Cannolis

Anna had really wanted to look professional for her very first therapy session, but as she went through her closet all she had was that fluffy white dress her mother had made her wear to a bar mitzvah. Desperate, she had invaded her mother's closet, trying on a skirt and a blouse that hung down to her ankles. She looked in the mirror and shook her head. *I look like Barbara Walters.* So she slipped her jeans back on and headed downstairs.

Anna exited the elevator. "Percy, when my patient gets here, just send him into my office."

"Of course, Miss Anna. And I will be here working on my book!" Percy replied with a wink.

Anna sat down at her office desk, which was really an old TV stand covered with one of her mother's silk scarves, and set to work reading her English-comprehension homework, when there was a knock at the door.

"Come in."

The door swung open, and one of the largest men Anna had ever seen filled the doorway.

He was both tall and wide, and wore a pair of dark sunglasses and an old suit that seemed two sizes too small on him.

"That Irish guy told me I'd find you here?" he said in a voice that wasn't as deep as you would expect.

"Come in," Anna smiled. "Take a seat. You must be Mr. Folgers who I talked to on the phone?"

"Huh? Oh yeah. Yeah, that's me, Mr. Folgers," the large man said with a nervous laugh, taking his sunglasses off as he positioned himself on the sofa. He looked around the room, which seemed much smaller when he filled it. Now that he was closer Anna noticed that he also had a large, crooked nose, and his hair was bleached platinum blonde except for where his dark roots were beginning to show.

"Hey, you're real small!" he exclaimed, turning to her.

Anna cleared her throat uneasily. "So, Mr. Folgers, why are you here today?" she asked, trying to sound as professional as possible.

"Like I said on the phone, I'm messed-up!"

"Do you mean that you're confused?"

"Yeah, I guess. I don't know. I'm just messed-up, ya know? In my head." And he raised one of his tremendous hands and pointed to his head. "And I'd like to be, you know, normal."

"Can you describe to me some problems you're having?" Anna said calmly.

"Well, like the other day, I was walkin' into this deli, because I really wanted a chocolate cannoli."

"What's a cannoli?"

"You've never had a cannoli?!" Mr. Folgers boomed. "It's only the best dessert on the face of this earth! That's it. I'm gonna bring you some cannolis!"

"So you were saying?"

"Oh, yeah! So I walked in this deli, and I say to the guy behind the counter, 'Eh! Gimme a chocolate cannoli!' So he hands me a cream puff, a round little cream puff, which doesn't look anything like a chocolate canolli. So I say again, 'Gimme a chocolate cannoli.' So he hands me a cheese danish. A freakin' cheese danish when I asked for a cannoli! So I start gettin' real mad, because this guy's trying to rip me off. Me! Who does he think he is? So I grab him by the collar, pull him over the counter, and throw him across the room."

Anna bit her lip. "So, um—you have some anger-management issues, Mr. Folgers."

"Yeah, that's what my ma always used to say."

"Did you tell your mother what happened at the bakery?"

"No, she left when I was four."

Anna gulped. "So you were even angry at *four?*"

"Oh, yeah, I beat up the whole neighborhood. I like to break things." Mr. Folgers smiled, his lips parting to reveal large, yellow teeth.

Anna took a deep breath and forced herself to continue on with the session.

"What does it feel like when you feel yourself getting angry, Mr. Folgers? Maybe there's something you can do to calm yourself down before you—you throw someone."

"Well," Mr. Folgers said, his large face thoughtful. "At first I start to get annoyed. Then I start getting real mad, and my chest gets all tight and I start seeing these red dots dancin' around my eyes. After a little bit, all I see is red, and I just wanna break something, to rip it open and tear it apart!" The large man had come forward on the sofa, and Anna could see the veins popping out in his neck as he got more and more heated.

"OK. Very good," she said calmly, trying to relax the large man. "Let me ask you another question. What is something that makes you feel good?"

"Uh, cannolis."

"OK, great! Mr. Folgers, when you start to get that annoyed feeling, I want you to breathe deeply and picture a delicious chocolate cannoli, count to ten and then walk away."

"Hmm. That's pretty good!" the large man said, crossing his long legs. Anna watched as he rested his shoe on his opposite knee. His feet were just as big as the rest of him, and his shoes were suede and a lovely shade of purple.

Purple! All of a sudden, Anna's heart skipped a beat. *Purple suede shoes!* Anna broke out into a fit of coughing.

"Hey, Anna. You OK?" said Mr. Folgers.

"Yes," she managed, studying the man across from her as everything began to fall into place: the dark sunglasses, the bleached hair, the ill-fitting suit. It was all a bad disguise. "Well, Mr. Folgers, time's up."

"Awww. I never knew therapy would be so much fun. If I had known, I would've gone when I was four!" He stood to his full height, and then with one large stride he was standing in the doorway again.

"Yeah, so we gotta do this again soon. I feel healed!"

Anna smiled weakly. "Is there a number where I can reach you at to schedule our next appointment, Mr. Folgers?" she asked casually.

"No. I'll call you."

And with that, Donny "the Meatball" Fratelli walked out of Anna's office.

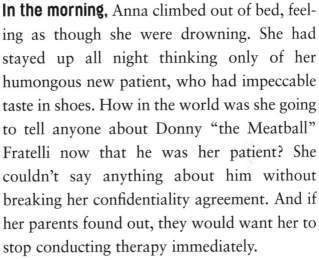

CHAPTER 20

Confidentiality

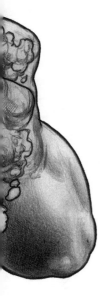

In the morning, Anna climbed out of bed, feeling as though she were drowning. She had stayed up all night thinking only of her humongous new patient, who had impeccable taste in shoes. How in the world was she going to tell anyone about Donny "the Meatball" Fratelli now that he was her patient? She couldn't say anything about him without breaking her confidentiality agreement. And if her parents found out, they would want her to stop conducting therapy immediately.

At school, Anna made a beeline straight to Ms. Sinclair's room. She gave the open door a light tap before stepping inside. "Ms. Sinclair?"

"Anna, what a pleasant surprise!" Ms. Sinclair was leaning on the windowsill, a mug of coffee in her hand. "How are those books I've lent you?"

"Good. They're good." Anna chewed her lower lip. "How's your sister?"

Ms. Sinclair's eyes dulled a little. "Oh, she's...well, we're all trying to take it day by day. I plan on visiting her at the hospital this weekend." Ms. Sinclair smiled sadly at Anna. "Thank you for asking."

For a moment, Anna debated telling Ms. Sinclair about the old abandoned Bendox gym and the men with machine guns—she wanted to tell her something, anything, to put her mind at ease. But she still didn't know how it all involved Mrs. Summer, and connected back to Mr. Who. There were still too many unanswered questions.

"So how's therapy coming along?"

Anna took a deep breath. "Well, I sort of wanted to ask you something...you know, about the confidentiality agreement? A shrink can't tell anyone who her patients are, right? And she can't discuss anything that goes on in sessions with anyone else. It's like a secret between the shrink and the patient, right?"

Ms. Sinclair looked at Anna carefully and then put her coffee mug down.

"Anna, a good therapist never breaks the confidentiality agreement, but if you feel like you can't handle a patient or don't want to, you have a right to refer them elsewhere. Promise me, Anna, if a patient is making you feel uncomfortable you'll send them elsewhere. You have that right."

Anna nodded, knowing full well that she couldn't refer Donny "the Meatball" Fratelli elsewhere; she had to take care of this problem herself and not dump it in someone else's lap. Especially if they didn't know Mr. Folgers *wasn't* Mr. Folgers.

Anna stuck around a couple more minutes and chatted with Ms. Sinclair about Parents' Day, which was coming up on Wednesday. She told Ms. Sinclair that she didn't think her parents were going to make it because they were tied up with work.

"Well, if your parents can't come, I'll be happy to walk around with you and talk to your teachers," Ms. Sinclair suggested.

Anna smiled, but deep down she wished her parents would come.

The afternoon was filled with constant reminders that Parents' Day was right around the corner. No matter how hard Anna tried to avoid it, in all of her classes the teachers were clamoring to prepare something special. Ms. Musashi even stopped Anna after math to ask her what color she thought she should wear for the special event. Absentmindedly, Anna had answered purple suede.

"What's the big deal about stupid Parents' Day anyway?" she muttered to Quenton.

Quenton just threw her a sad glance. He knew her parents probably weren't going to make it.

"I mean, it's just one lame day out of the year," Anna mumbled, opening her locker. "I don't see everyone getting all worked up over Flag Day or Groundhog Day or May Day—" She broke off as a thin black folder fell forward, a blood-red message scrawled on the front of it: GET THAT TURD!

Anna sighed with relief. Now that Clea's photographs were here, she could finally visit Principal Rollins and clear her name once and for all! Saying bye to Quenton, Anna marched across the hall and raised a hand to the perfectly polished wooden door. But just as she was about to knock, the door jerked open.

"Miss Smudge," crooned Thaddeus T. Rollins, "just the person I've been wanting to see. Come in."

Bravely, she stepped inside the office and took a seat in a big wooden chair across from the principal's perfectly polished wooden desk—the desk she had hidden under yesterday.

"Now," Mr. Rollins said, taking a seat across from her. "I hear you've become quite the troublemaker."

"Which is what I wanted to discuss with you, Mr. Rollins," said Anna calmly. "You see, it's not me who's the troublemaker." She slapped Clea's black folder onto the desk. "It's Jacob Pierce. I have the proof right here."

Mr. Rollins opened the folder and began to sift through the photos: Jacob bent over his sneakers and taking a melted Hershey bar out of his sock; Jacob wiping the chocolate on his hands; Jacob glancing around the room suspiciously; Jacob taunting Anna and smiling evilly; and finally a shot of him grabbing her with his dirty hands. All of the photos were in perfect focus and told the story like illustrations in a book.

When he finally looked up Mr. Rollins's face was the color of Jacob's hair. "Well, Miss Smudge," he said in a curt voice, "I guess I owe you an apology."

"It wasn't your fault," Anna replied. "Jacob pulled one over on everyone. I just wanted the truth to be known."

Mr. Rollins nodded. "Well, if it's any consolation, I'll explain the situation to your teachers this afternoon."

Pure relief washed through Anna.

"This kind of thing should not go on at the Bendox School of Excellence!" Mr. Rollins continued, scribbling something on his desk. "I will make sure to see this Pierce boy as soon as I can and, of course, contact his parents."

Anna sat up a little straighter, clutching both hands in her lap. *Don't say it. Don't say it!* she thought.

"I will also be sure to call your parents and explain this awful and very unfortunate misunderstanding to them as well."

He said it. Now her parents would find out about the message she had erased.

Mr. Rollins reached for his gold-rimmed spectacles. "I did leave a message with your parents, though, and they still haven't gotten back to me."

"Well, my father's awfully busy right now. He and my mother have this really, really big, important business deal going down. I mean, they hardly even have time to eat or sleep!" *Or to spend time with me,* Anna thought glumly.

"Indeed? Not even to return one little phone call?"

Anna shrugged.

Thaddeus T. Rollins shut the black folder and tucked it into the bowels of his desk. "Well, I guess that settles the matter. You may be excused, Miss Smudge."

A New Friend

The day came crashing to an end like a semi truck with no brakes. Anna tramped down the hallway, trying to avoid the whispers and penetrating stares of her classmates. All afternoon, kids from all grades had clamored to schedule appointments; Anna's binder was now filled to the brim with messy scribbling, and already she was completely booked until next month!

Feeling utterly overwhelmed, she wove her way through a crowd surrounding Rachel's new bulletin board, *The Riley News*. Rachel stood in the center of the large cluster, hanging a new article: Mrs. Summer: The Art, the Life, the Tragedy.

When Rachel saw Anna, she lifted her chin and mouthed, "Tonight!"

Anna nodded back and tried to swallow the large lump in her throat. Yes, tonight was the night they would sneak inside the old Bendox gym. As if having a dangerous criminal as a patient and a ton of extra blackmail homework wasn't enough, now she had to deal with breaking into an armed facility.

Anna shoved the bathroom door open and bent over the sink, trying to breathe, trying not the think about the giant purple mess she was in. She heard shuffling and looked up to see Amy hovering timidly by the sink. "Hi, Anna. I was wondering if I could talk to you about something."

Suddenly the bathroom door slammed open and a gaggle of girls marched in. "Are you Anna Smudge?" demanded a tiny third-grader.

Anna shot Amy a pained look and reluctantly nodded her head.

"'Cause I need therapy, like, now! My parents only let me watch a half-hour of TV a night, and my favorite program is an hour long. I have to turn it off right in the middle, and then next week I don't know what's going on."

"Oh, yeah?" cut in a chubby girl with braces. "My dad makes me go to the dentist every six months! He's really abusive like that."

"Well, my mom won't even let me wear her diamonds to school! Why have kids, then? You know what I mean?"

"Yes, well, I don't conduct therapy in the bathroom," Anna walked the group toward the door. "If you could just call to schedule appointments. Thanks, looking forward to hearing from you," she said, nudging them outside and barricading the door with a large garbage bin. Then she slid onto the floor in a puddle of stress.

"It's just too much," she muttered. "I can't handle it all."

"Is there something wrong?" Amy looked down at Anna, her face filled with concern.

"Yeah, I'm a mess! I'm supposed to be this big shrink, and I can barely handle my own problems. I mean, the phone calls and appointments are endless. And I have twice as much homework as everyone else. And I can hardly even get the homework done because I'm so busy scheduling appointments!"Anna exhaled. "I'm sorry, Amy, I don't mean to unload on you. Did you say there was something you wanted to talk to me about?"

"No...It's nothing, really." Amy looked very worried. "It can wait until later. But is there any way I can help?"

The bathroom doorknob began to turn back and forth. "Anna Smudge?" called a muffled voice. "It's me, Jeffrey Capshew! Barbara Baskerville kissed me, and now I think I have terminal cooties!"

Anna looked at Amy and smiled weakly. "What did you have in mind?"

"Well, I have a Blackberry and unlimited minutes." Amy blushed. "I'm adopted, so I guess my parents over-compensate, you know? I think they hope it might make me a little more sociable." Amy pointed towards the inky mess of scribbles that spilled out of Anna's binder. "But I'm very organized, and it's much easier for me to talk to people on the phone than in person. I could take messages and schedule appointments for you?"

"Well, if you *want* to, Amy. That would make life so much easier! I could forward my calls to you. Then you can just email me my schedule."

Amy nodded enthusiastically. "It'll be like I'm your sec-retary!" She stared down at the floor, embarrassed. "Anyway, I'd really like to help you, Anna. I mean, you've helped practically everyone."

Not everyone, Anna thought, remembering the look of misery on poor Simon Spektor's face.

.◦.

On her way downtown to the dreaded old gym, Anna made one last important stop. She stepped through the beautiful archway of a magnificent white townhouse and gave the enormous brass door knocker a rap. It had been nagging at her ever since that day on the subway—Simon was the one person she couldn't seem to help.

"Yes, can I help you?" A tall, severe-looking woman wearing a fitted pinstriped suit answered the door.

"Um, hi," Anna said, suddenly nervous. "I'm here to see Simon. You see, he wasn't in school today, and I wanted to make sure he was OK."

The tall woman surveyed Anna coldly. "I'm sorry, but Simon's very sick. He's upstairs with the doctor. He's not seeing anyone right now."

"Oh." Anna shuffled awkwardly on her feet, and then she held out a small brown bag. "I brought him some chicken soup from the Polish place on the corner. It's homemade."

The woman took the soup from Anna. "Thank you. I'll be sure to tell Simon you came by."

"Are you...his mother?" Anna blurted out.

The tall woman glared down at Anna, who had the sudden urge to run away.

"No," the woman replied in a crisp voice. "My name is Ms. Dankashane. I'm the family's assistant."

"Oh." Anna turned to leave. "Well, I should get going."

"Are you Anna?" Ms. Dankashane asked suddenly.

Astonished, Anna merely nodded.

"Simon talks about you. He says you're always trying to make him feel better."

Anna flushed, and quickly looked down at her shoes. "Yeah, and I haven't really helped at all. I've just acted like a jerk, really."

"Simon has nothing but the best of things to say about you. He has told me many times over many meals that you are an exemplary person. A very good *friend*."

Surprised, Anna looked back up.

"Simon's a very lonely boy," Ms. Dankashane said quietly. "I've been with the family for a long time, and through it all Simon has always suffered with his health. Because of that, I'm afraid he has no friends at all—aside from you, that is. Thank you for being so kind to him."

Ms. Dankashane cleared her throat and stepped backward into a rich marble foyer trimmed with gold. "It was nice to finally meet a friend of Simon's. He will be very glad to hear you came by."

And with that, she shut the door.

CHAPTER 22

The Door Beneath the Bleachers

A bright crescent moon hung low in the night sky. Anna stood in the dark, deserted playground behind the old Bendox gym, her eyes fearfully darting around at the shadows.

"Ugh! It smells like fifty-year-old Underoos."

"That's because it's an old laundry chute, dummy."

"Hurry, Quenton, this place is freaking me out!"

Anna pointed her flashlight at a tiny opening in the gym wall and watched as her friends wedged themselves through one by one. She wished they would hurry.

"Hey, want me to be the last one through?"

Anna turned to see Clea and shook her head. "No, it's OK. By the way, thanks for coming."

"No prob. Like I said, Mrs. Summer got me started in photography. I owe her huge." Clea rolled up the sleeves of her black turtleneck—she was dressed like a ninja. "See you on the other side, compadre," she whispered, and disappeared into the wall.

Anna stood alone. A rusty swing creaked eerily in the wind and a twig snapped someplace nearby. She bolted toward the tiny opening, pushing herself through, and before she knew it she was sliding down a rusty chute and landing with a soft plop in an old pile of laundry.

"It's the old locker room," whispered Todd, extending a hand to help her up.

Anna glanced around at the cobweb-covered lockers and shower stalls before following the others. They had just slipped through the doorway and into the darkened gym, creeping as quietly as they could, when suddenly Quenton's hands shot up into the air. "We surrender peacefully! We surrender peacefully!"

Gasping, they found themselves staring up into the end of a large cannon barrel. It hovered in the air, pointing toward their heads like a giant deadly finger. They quickly mimicked Quenton, raising their arms and squeezing their eyes shut tight...and waited.

"I'm too young to die," whimpered Quenton. "I haven't even tried Russian caviar yet."

A long moment passed, but still nothing happened. Anna's arms were getting heavy; she wasn't sure how much longer she could hold them up. She heard a couple sniffles and some nervous shuffling, and then...

"Guys, it's empty." Clea peered up at the army tank sitting in the middle of the basketball court like an enormous steel mountain.

Anna breathed a sigh of relief, her arms collapsing to her sides.

"OK, I think I want to turn back now," squeaked Rachel.

Clea took a small, dark object from her pocket. "Stick with me. I've got pepper spray. Just aim for the eyes, kick below the belt, and run as fast as you can yelling, 'FIRE!' Works every time."

Bravely, Rachel nodded and edged closer to Clea.

"Something is inside this building, and we're going to find out what it is!" Todd gathered them together in a huddle. "We need to split up. That way we'll be able to search the building quicker. Be as quiet as possible, and stick to the outer walls like peanut butter. Let's meet back here in ten minutes."

Everyone nodded, and they went their separate ways. Todd disappeared behind a tall stack of mats; Quenton entered a small coach's office; Rachel vanished into a large equipment closet; and Clea started for a door on the opposite end of the room.

Now alone, Anna felt a prickle of fear. She looked around at the deserted gym. Aside from the massive army tank, it was as if everything had frozen in time—the floors were old scratched wood, two ragged basketball nets hung on either side of the silent, empty court, and all of the twenty-year old gym equipment was neatly stacked against the walls. Wondering where to explore first, Anna's gaze finally rested on the bleachers covering the far wall.

She stooped to enter the inky blackness beneath the slatted wooden steps. Her feet crunched on old broken Coke bottles and kicked aside pages of long-discarded homework. As she bent down to scrape a gob of bubble gum off her shoe, something caught her eye. There was a sliver of light. And as Anna crept towards it she was surprised to find—a door? What was a door doing under here? Heart pounding, she slowly pushed it open and stepped out into a long white-tiled corridor flooded with flourescent light.

Sticking close to the wall, she began to walk...and walk.... It seemed like the corridor went on forever, sloping slightly and extending deep below the gym. Anna glanced behind her as her exit grew farther and farther away. Bright yellow warning signs plastered along the walls read:

Looking at the signs, Anna felt her stomach drop. What were they keeping down here? Maybe she shouldn't be exploring alone. Maybe she should go back and tell her friends...

Just then, the heavy clomp of boots sounded from the far end of the hallway. Someone was coming around the corner! Panicking, Anna flattened herself against the white-tiled wall. *Who am I kidding?* she thought. *I'm going to stick out like a sore thumb.*

The boots plodded closer. Desperately, Anna looked a few feet away and saw two swinging doors with more DANGER signs plastered over the windows. Without a second thought, she dodged through the doors on her hands and knees.

.•.

She was in a gleaming white laboratory filled with shiny metallic equipment. Anna ducked beneath a small cart littered with test tubes and beakers and watched as people in white lab coats scurried around, taking measurements, typing data into computers, and peering into microscopes. A woman walked right by her, carrying a vial of dark liquid. She pressed a keypad on the wall, and a metal tray popped out of a refrigerated vault. After placing the vial into a frozen carrier and resealing the door, the woman joined two other scientists near a strange structure in the center of the room.

Anna quietly wheeled her cart closer and peeked her head out. In back of the scientists was a small tent-like chamber made entirely of plastic.

Suddenly, an alarm began to blare and red lights flashed on and off. There was a loud hiss, like someone was letting all the air out of a tire, and an airlock on the side of the small plastic tent opened. Two figures stumbled out;

they had on yellow astronaut-looking suits—thick yellow gloves, tall boots, and bulky helmets complete with a breathing apparatus.

"Ernie's contaminated!" yelled a tinny voice over the alarm.

"He's got a tear in his glove!" said the other suited man. Then he lifted a helmet off his head—and looked directly at Anna.

.●.

She ran, skidding on the white slippery floor, pushing off on the white-tiled walls. Something was in that sealed plastic room. Something dangerous! Gasping for breath, Anna nearly missed the door—it blended into the white wall almost like it wasn't there. She cranked it open, scrambling through, and then she was underneath the bleachers once again, racing out onto the gym floor only to find an odd sort of...basketball game?

"Touchdown! Home run!" shouted Quenton, blowing his whistle.

Todd was dribbling a basketball across the gym while Clea raised her hands in the air trying to block him. Two large guards awkwardly fumbled over all kinds of balls rolling around on the floor, trying to catch Todd. Todd quickly passed the ball to Rachel, who ran with it across the court, threw it over her head, and missed the basket terribly.

"Goal! Strike!" cried Quenton, blowing his whistle and kicking some more soccer balls onto the court.

"Stop! We order you to stop!" shouted one of the guards, but the shrill cry of Quenton's whistle drowned him out.

"Hey guy, I told you! If you wanna play, you should've tried out for the team in September along with everyone else. Right, Anna?" Quenton looked at Anna and did a double take.

"Anna!" Rachel hissed, racing over and grabbing her arm. "Where on earth have you been? We've been trying to distract these guys. We've been—"

There was the deafening blast of a horn. Anna huddled into Rachel, holding her ears. An intimidating man in a black suit and dark glasses was standing by the doorway holding an air horn.

"What is the meaning of this?"

He addressed the question to the two guards, who were standing in the middle of the gym, looking mystified. Soccer balls, volleyballs, and basketballs rolled around their feet.

"Hey, we're trying to play some ball here!" Quenton stepped forward. "Is this a gym or what?"

"No, not anymore," the man said. "This building is under construction. I'm not sure how you kids got in here..." Anna couldn't see the man's eyes, but she could tell he was glaring at the two guards. "But you'll have to find somewhere else to play."

"This is so screwed-up! This is just so screwed-up!"

"I know," agreed Rachel solemnly. "It sounds like something really dangerous is being held in that room."

"No, I mean this." Quenton held up his snifter glass. "I ordered a brandy, but I'm pretty sure this is apple juice."

They all sat crammed in a corner table of a loud, seedy bar by the Seaport, sipping sodas and speculating about what was being kept in the small plastic room.

"It was completely sealed," said Anna. "I mean, there was no door. Just this airlock thing. And the men who came out were wearing these bulky yellow suits—"

"Hazmat suits," said Quenton matter-of-factly.

"What?"

"You remember, the stuff people wear to protect them from deadly viruses—a hazardous-materials suit. And that sealed plastic room—probably a 'clean room.'"

Quenton took a sip of apple juice. Everyone just stared at him.

"What? I watch a lot of cable."

"So the CIA—I mean that guy was definitely CIA, right, Quenton? They must be holding something really dangerous—and really contagious—in that clean room," said Todd.

"Probably a biological weapon," said Quenton, raising his snifter and signaling to the bartender. "Make it a double!" he called out.

"A biological weapon," Anna repeated, feeling her stomach drop all the way down to the floor. She wasn't exactly sure what that was, but it didn't sound pleasant.

"A bioweapon, otherwise known as germ warfare, is the illegal use of a dangerous virus or bacterium as a weapon," Rachel prattled on, reading from her phone's encyclopedia. "If released, the effect can be devastating. Millions of people can become infected and d-die." She broke off, her face becoming pale.

They all grew very quiet. People on the other end of the bar swayed and sang drunkenly, sloshing their mugs to and fro, but Anna just felt ill.

"Guys," Quenton's voice was unusually soft. "I think I know why Uncle Brian built that special airtight box for Mr. Who." He looked up, his eyes large and fearful. "Mr. Who is going to use the box to steal the bioweapon."

"What are we going to do?" asked Todd quietly.

"What *can* we do?" cried Quenton. "No one thinks the guy is even real. And we're kids, remember? Who would listen to us anyway?"

Clea slammed her fist onto the tabletop. "It's up to us, then. We have to catch Mr. Who."

"Sure," chimed Quenton enthusiastically. "Tomorrow at noon is good for me!" Then he rolled his eyes and snorted. "I mean, who're we kidding? The only thing we can catch is a cold."

"It's Mr. Pierce. He's Mr. Who. I just know he is," said Anna.

"But can you prove it?" pointed out Todd.

"He's hired Donny 'the Meatball' Fratelli!"

"But so have a lot of shady folks," said Rachel. "Look

around, Anna. Anyone in here could be Mr. Who! No one knows what he even looks like. He could be your bartender or your mailman or—"

"—the father of the Turd," finished Clea. She looked at Anna. "I think it's him too. So the question is: how are we gonna get him?"

"I don't know, but if I don't sneak back home soon, I'll be in a world without cable." Quenton glanced at his watch and chugged the rest of his apple juice in one large gulp.

"And my mom will ground me until I'm thirteen," agreed Rachel, rising from her seat. "We'll have to figure this out later."

"Yeah, the bioweapon is safe for now. Those Army guys have it well protected."

Everyone quickly rose from the table, nodding and mumbling about getting home...except Anna. She sat glumly, thinking about how her parents probably wouldn't even notice she was gone.

Unacceptable Behavior

Anna couldn't stop thinking about the bio-weapon. At least the CIA had it locked up and guarded. She dumped her backpack in the foyer and started toward the kitchen for a late-night snack but was stopped in her tracks.

"Anna, could you please come in here?"

Anna's heart skipped a beat.

"Anna!" her mother's voice called again. "Your father and I would like to discuss something with you."

Anna walked to the entrance of her father's study, her legs felt weak.

"Come sit down."

Both her parents were sitting on the plush velvet sofa and had an empty chair positioned in front of them. She took a seat in the chair, feeling like she sat under a spotlight.

"Anna," her father said, and she could hear the disappointment in his voice. "We got a phone call from your principal today."

Anna swallowed fearfully.

"Do you have anything you'd like to tell us?"

Anna just sat in the chair, facing both of her parents who stared at her expectantly.

"Anna, your father is talking to you," her mother said sharply.

Anna felt her eyes begin to well up.

"Anna, Principal Rollins called to apologize for his initial message. A message I never received. Do you know what happened to it?"

Silence. Nothing but the ticking of the large grandfather clock in the corner and Anna's heavy breathing. It was as if she could hear every little thing going on inside her body—her heart pounding, her stomach gurgling.

"Anna, your father asked you a question. Do you know what happened to Principal Rollins's message?"

Anna shook her head.

"I think you do," her father said softly.

"This is unacceptable behavior," her mother said, rising angrily from the sofa. "It is just unacceptable! Did we raise you to do things like this? To erase messages, messages that weren't yours? To lie?"

"Anna," her father said, also rising from the sofa and pacing the Oriental rug so that he and her mother were now like two sharks circling her chair. "Erasing messages to hide the fact that you were in trouble is quite unacceptable."

"Your father could have lost an important job! An important client! Why would you do that to your father, who works so hard to provide for you? Why?"

Anna felt hot tears spring to her eyes and slowly drip

down her cheeks. She felt as if her face was on fire and her chest was being squeezed.

"Answer me."

"Do you have anything to say for yourself, young lady?"

"Why would you try to hide something like that from us?"

"Because!" Anna screamed, rising from the chair on shaky legs. "I never see you! It's as if I don't exist! And I didn't want the little attention I do get from you to be about something I did wrong! Like right now! So I erased Daddy's stupid message. I don't care. I hate you! I hate you!" And she ran from the study, up the stairs, and slammed the door to her room and locked it.

A little while later, there was a knock on the door.

"Anna?"

There was no answer.

"Anna, we're leaving first thing in the morning for our business trip. We'll talk about this when we get back."

Footsteps sounded down the hall.

Anna lay sprawled on her bed with her head buried in her pillow. She had exhausted herself so much downstairs that she had dozed off and now awoke to stare at the clock. It was almost midnight.

She rose and padded into the bathroom to wash her puffy face. Hungry for food and the crisp night air, she tip-toed down the stairs, carrying her shoes in her hands so that she wouldn't make any noise. She didn't put her shoes back on until she was safely in the elevator. And then she was outside, among the traffic and pedestrians, walking toward a dingy all-night falafel stand on First Avenue while ruminating on the bioweapon and what Mr. Who's plan to steal it could possibly be.

Anna ordered a super falafel without the spicy peppers and ate as she walked back to her building. Even without the peppers, her insides burned with guilt. She hadn't handled the situation with her parents very well; she had said so many hurtful things. But in an odd way, she felt like a huge weight had been lifted. The truth was out. She no longer had to worry about her blackmailer—the worst had finally happened.

Anna gritted her teeth. There was only one thing to do now. No one knew that her parents had found out about the missing message. Monday morning Anna would drop off the extra homework in Grand Central Station as usual, but this time she would hide out. This time she would catch red-faced Jacob Pierce red-handed.

CHAPTER 24

An Unlikely Suspect

Grand Central Station was a zoo.

Anna hid behind the massive clock, watching for Jacob. She had just slipped a bunch of blank sheets of paper onto the shelf of the Currency Exchange Booth. She didn't really have a plan. She had no idea what she was going to say to Jacob and his Cheshire-cat smile once she faced him. All she knew was that facing him was something she had to do.

Where is he?

Just then, a small figure shot through a clump of businessmen. Anna craned her neck, eager for a glimpse of Jacob—a sneaker or a backpack—but the crowd was thickly packed and her view was obscured.

Anna crept out from behind the clock and carefully wove her way through the swarm, eager to reach the booth. She was almost there, almost at the metal shelf.

She could see a figure leaning over it. Anna reached a hand out and—

"Amy?"

Amy Lerner whirled around to face Anna, a sheet of paper clutched in her hand.

"Amy, w-what are doing...here?" Anna could barely get the words to leave her mouth.

Amy just stood there, doe-eyed and frightened.

"You're my blackmailer?" Anna gasped. "But why?"

"I tried to tell you," Amy said softly, gazing at the ground. "I tried to talk to you...but you seemed so—so stressed out."

"Of course I was stressed out!" Anna cried. "I was being blackmailed!"

People walking by shot them a backward glance, but Anna didn't care.

"Why, Amy? I thought you were my friend. And then you did that stuff to help me out..."

Amy stared at the floor of Grand Central as if it were the most engrossing thing in the world. And just when Anna thought she was going to have to shake the girl, a soft voice started to speak:

"Roselyn made me do it. Well, she didn't make me, but she told me to. It all started after you pulled Jacob's hair in math class, the day you fought back. I couldn't believe you did that. I thought you were so brave. But I couldn't tell Roselyn that. After all, Jacob is her cousin, and she was so mad! She told me to sneak out after you and listen in on what Principal Rollins said. No one even noticed I was gone—probably because no one even notices when I'm there. So I overheard Principal Rollins say that he left a message on your father's answering machine, and when I told Roselyn...she got very excited."

Anna had to lean in to hear Amy as she talked more than Anna had ever heard her talk before. When she spoke, her voice was as soft as a whisper, and her eyes remained glued to the floor.

"Roselyn got this voice changer from Jacob's dad—it makes your voice sound all strange and scary. After school we called you, and she whispered to me what to say. Then Roselyn got the idea that she could get you to do her homework. She made me write out the notes because I have neat handwriting. Then she had you leave the home-work at Grand Central Station for me to pick up because I live on Forty-sixth Street, and I always take the subway from here to get to school. I-I..."

Amy's soft voice broke, and a tear splashed onto the floor of Grand Central Station as people hurried by, their shoes clicking loudly. "I'm so sorry, Anna. I knew it was wrong. I hate the things Roselyn does to people, but she said if I didn't do it she wouldn't be my friend anymore, and then—then I'd be alone."

At that, Amy looked up, her brown eyes glassy and her cheeks flushed pink. "It was before I knew you—before you approached me that day. I couldn't believe it when you just came over and started talking to me." She looked down at the ground again and she said, in a voice so quiet it was almost lost in the melee, "It was before I knew how wonderful you are."

A long moment passed. A businessman pushed by Anna, a group of tourists chatted loudly in German, and a baby nearby began to wail.

"Look, Amy," Anna said, glancing around uncomfortably. "It's still really early. Let's go someplace a little quieter."

"You still want to go somewhere with *me?*" Amy's tears dripped down her cheeks like tiny crystals.

Anna put her arm around the girl and said, "C'mon, let's get some grub."

.●.

Anna and Amy sat under an archway lined with tiny lights in the Oyster Bar Restaurant, eating chilled seafood from a silver platter.

"More lemonade, Anna?" asked their waiter, grinning widely as he refilled her glass. "Saved my marriage, you did. For twenty-three years I'd been married to a screaming yeti, and after seeing you—it's like we're newlyweds again!" He did a little jig across the dining room and disappeared into the kitchen.

Amy smiled at Anna, a look of excitement on her tear-streaked face. "Gosh, Anna, it's like everyone in Manhattan's your patient!" Then she looked down, playing with the corner of her tablecloth. "Anna, do you still want me to be your secretary?"

"Amy, you're the best secretary I've ever had!"

"Um, I'm the *only* secretary you've ever had."

Anna giggled but then thought of something. "So, Roselyn got the voice changer from Jacob's dad, huh? Are you guys over at Jacob's a lot?"

Amy nodded. "Yeah, sometimes. But I don't like it over there. There's a lot of scary people."

"Amy, let me ask you something." Anna lowered her voice. "Do you think Mr. Pierce is Mr. Who?"

Amy thought for a moment and then nodded knowingly. "He certainly is mean enough."

Anna wandered down the sidewalk, clutching a bag of desserts that she and Amy had been too stuffed to finish. All she could think of was her next appointment with the Meatball. It was this afternoon. She *had* to get more information out of him. She had to find out when Mr. Who was planning on stealing the bioweapon, and how. Anna clenched her fists. If she could just get Donny to tell her whether Mr. Who was really Mr. Pierce...

She was so deep in thought that she almost didn't notice the short figure sitting on the front stoop of a brownstone, hunched over a handheld video game, a large tissue box propped on the step next to him.

"Simon!" Anna called, a new spring to her step. She was determined to help this boy if it was the last thing she did. If she couldn't help Simon, then she couldn't consider herself a shrink at all.

Surprised, Simon briefly glanced up from his game.

"Can I join you?" Anna asked.

"If you want to risk catching Q Fever." he replied in his nasal voice.

"Q Fever?" Anna repeated.

"Yeah, it's a very rare disease that animals get. I think I might have caught it over the weekend when I went looking for my little brother at the zoo. But I'm not sure. I have to see Dr. Fanconi this afternoon."

Not knowing quite what to say, Anna sat down on the stoop next to the sniffling boy. "I met Ms. Dankashane."

"Yeah," Simon said, his eyes still glued to his game. Then he looked up and smiled. "She told me you came by. Thanks."

"Sure thing," Anna grinned. "So what are you playing?"

"It's my new game player. I got it 'cause I'm waiting in doctors' offices a lot. This one has an Internet connection so I can get on MMORPGs."

"MMORPGs?" Anna repeated.

"Yeah, a 'massively multiplayer online role-playing game,' where you get to play against people all over the world. You know the big Cyber Kingdom war? Well, I was the one who got the flag down and let the West Kingdom into the castle."

Anna had no idea what Simon was talking about, but she nodded her head anyway. "That's cool. I don't really know much about video games."

Simon sat up a little straighter. "Well, I used to be into the games where you blast things, but then I got really into these other games where you have to figure things out and solve riddles and stuff—like you have to be able to tell who's your enemy and who's not, and step back and see the bigger picture. It's not just shooting people with guns and stuff."

Anna smiled weakly. "How did you get into all of this?"

"I'm around adults a lot," Simon said in his quiet, nasal voice. "You know doctors, nurses, and you met Ms. Dankashane...people like that. So I'm not really good at talking to people my own age. I guess that's why I play a lot of games."

"Well, people are just people. All you have to do is talk. Look how well you're doing with me."

Simon nodded. "Yeah, I guess you're right."

Anna thought of something. "Simon, since you like games so much maybe you should start looking at real life like one big game. That way you'll be braver! And then you'll talk to more people!"

Simon's eyes opened up wide behind his glasses, and he nodded enthusiastically. "That's a good idea," he said. "A game. All one big game."

"Here." Anna opened up her bag and took out a brownie. "Help yourself."

Simon shook his head. "No, I'm afraid the chocolate will make my acid reflux act up."

Anna hunched forward, her eyes sparkling. "Well, let's risk it. Just this once! What do you say?"

Simon stared back at Anna, a glint in his eyes. He pushed his heavily rimmed glasses up with a finger and said, "I guess I like the occasional risk."

Anna took one more brownie from the bag, and together they ate in silence. "Wow, this is so good!" Anna exclaimed.

"Mmm," Simon replied, chocolate lining the outside of his mouth.

Anna watched Simon momentarily forget about his tissue box and his portable game and enjoy his dessert and thought to herself, *It's too bad chocolate won't solve any of my problems.*

CHAPTER 25

The Last Hit

Anna fretfully waited in her office for Donny "the Meatball" Fratelli. She had to try to get as much information out of him as possible. She frantically tapped one foot, then the other, then both feet at one time, and then—

"Hey, Anna!" An immense frame filled the doorway. "I brought you some chocolate cannolis." Donny excitedly waved a paper bag in one hand. "You gotta have one!"

"Why thank you, Don—Mr. Folgers," Anna said. "I will definitely try one…a bit later. Shall we get started with our session?"

"No!" Donny "the Meatball" frowned. "Have one NOW!"

"OK." Anna quickly opened the bag, taking out a long pastry. She handed the other one to Donny and proceeded to take a bite. "Mmm. This is very good!" she said, forcing a smile.

"See?" Donny said proudly. "I told you you'd like 'em!" He pulled a spoon out of his pocket. Anna jumped back in fear.

"I like to scoop out the insides!" the large man exclaimed, digging the spoon into the creamy middle and eating the inside first.

Anna breathed a sigh of relief.

When they were finished with their cannolis, Anna sat back in her seat and began the session, trying to think of a way that she might be able to trick Donny.

"So Mr. Folgers, what have you been up to?"

"Well, um, my boss gave me a new hit—I mean, job."

Anna grimaced. "That's great. What does this job entail? Who are you working with, what do you have to do?"

"Well," Donny said, shifting his huge frame around on the sofa. "My boss wants me to meet this guy Wednesday night and hit—I mean, help him."

"Oh?" Anna said. "This man you're meeting to help... Mr...er...Mr..."

"Smudge," Donny answered matter-of-factly. "Mr. Smudge."

Anna's heart stopped.

She felt her legs turn to Jell-O and her arms to pudding. Her father! Mr. Who had a hit out on her father!

"Hey, Anna, you OK?"

Anna looked up at the large face peering down at her and tried to contain herself. She had to! Now was not the time to freak out. She had to find a way to get more information.

Anna sat up straight, clasping her shaking hands together. She looked Donny "the Meatball" Fratelli right in the eyes and said in a crisp voice, "Mr. Folgers, I don't think you're being honest with me. And if you don't tell me the *whole* truth during our sessions, I'm afraid I *cannot* help you get better."

The large man looked as if he was going to pop his top, his face turned as red as a beet, and the veins on his neck stood out like twigs, but Anna held her ground and stared the humongous man right in the eyes without looking away. "If you're *not* going to tell me everything, please leave. Our therapy sessions will end right here, right now."

Anna held her breath and waited to see what the humongous man on her sofa would do. She hoped he didn't use his spoon. Even more, she hoped he didn't leave. If he did, that would leave her with nothing!

Donny's face turned from bright red to pink and finally to a pale, peachy tone as he exhaled. "You're right, Anna. I've been a liar. A dirty, good-for-nothing-liar." He stared down at his large purple shoes as he spoke.

"My name's Donny. I'm really a hitman. I work for... Mr. Who."

"And why does Mr. Who want Mr. Smudge d-dead?"

"So that he can win this big-deal government shipping job. Mr. Who wants the government to use one of *his* ships, not one of Mr. Smudge's ships. The government is moving this thingy next weekend, I'm not sure what, but Mr. Who sure wants to get his hands on it, whatever it is."

Anna nodded, as everything began to click into place. The government contract her parents had been worried about—they must be planning to move the bioweapon somewhere safe. That was why they were keeping it in an abandoned school gym by the Seaport, so that it would be right by the water. But if they used one of Mr. Who's ships, he'd be able to sneak the weapon off in the special box Quenton's uncle, Dr. LeGrande, made for him. He'd be able to steal it right from under their noses!

Anna looked up at Donny, her heart pounding. She had to convince him not to carry out the hit.

"Donny, let me ask you something. Is this really what you wanted to be when you were younger?" Anna raised her eyebrows slowly. "A hitman?"

"No, it was never my dream." The large man slumped down on the sofa. "I don't wanna be a hitman no more," he whined. "That's why I started seeing you. You see, I wanna go to beauty school! I wanna do hair." Donny reached up and ruffled his bleached-blonde do.

Anna leaned forward. "So then *don't* be a hitman, Donny."

Donny tilted his chin up. "I'm not! I'm not gonna be no more!"

Anna breathed a sigh of relief.

"After this hit, I'm done. I'm outta the business!"

Anna sucked in a breath again. "But why even do this hit then?" she pushed. "Why not just start your new life immediately?"

"Because Mr. Who would kill me." For the first time, Donny "the Meatball" Fratelli looked petrified. "Mr. Who was real angry when he found out that I hadn't done the hit yet. You see, it all started when I left a message on Mr. Smudge's answering machine telling him to back out of the shipping job, but he never called back. What are you gonna do, ya know? Sometimes folks just don't return calls. Personally, I think that's very rude. So Mr. Who told me to kill him."

Anna clutched the arms of her chair. The message. The other message she had erased on her father's answering machine had been from Donny. By erasing that message, Anna had put a hit on her father's life.

"No, you don't mess with Mr. Who," Donny said gravely. "He'll know if you do. He'll know, and then when you least expect it...BAM!"

Anna jumped in her seat.

"But I called the Smudge guy again and set up a meeting for when he gets back in town Wednesday night. That's when I'm gonna do it." Donny raised his giant hand like a gun and then smiled. "After Wednesday night, I'm a new man!"

Anna sat in silence, not knowing what to say.

"So I'm doing good!" Donny "the Meatball" declared happily, standing up and almost hitting his large head on the low ceiling. "Soon I'll be an upstanding citizen! Right, Anna?"

·ö·

"I need to talk to the Chief of Police!" Anna insisted, standing on her tiptoes in front of the tall desk in Police

Precinct 19. "Please!" She tried to catch her breath. She had run the whole way over here.

"Now what seems to be the problem, little girl?" A tall, skinny officer stood behind the desk, organizing a teetering stack of papers, and eyed her impatiently.

"Donny 'the Meatball' Fratelli is going to kill my dad!" Anna blurted, trying to hold back her tears. "I have to talk to someone—the Chief—the whatever—right away!"

The officer placed the stack of papers down with a plop. "And where did you hear about Donny 'the Meatball'?"

Anna shook her head, trying to think, as her heart raced in her ears. "Um, I guess I first heard about him on the news."

"Well, next time turn the station." The officer returned to his paperwork.

"Listen, I need to see the Chief!" Anna cried, choking back a sob. "I need to see someone NOW! Donny is going to kill my dad! Don't you understand?" She could feel her hands begin to shake and quickly stuffed them in her pockets. "He works for Mr. Who. Mr. Who wants to steal this dangerous bioweapon from the government—" Anna broke off as she saw the screwy expression on the officer's face.

"OK," she said slowly. "Mr. Who isn't real. Got it. I know. But Donny 'the Meatball' Fratelli is real. He really exists, right? He's a famous hitman!"

Irritated, the officer glared at Anna. "And how do you know Donny 'the Meatball' is going to kill your dad?"

"He-he told me!"

"He told you," repeated the officer.

Anna nodded. "Yeah, he told me in one of our sessions. He's my patient. I'm a shrink."

"Oh, are you?" the officer smirked. "And Bugs Bunny is in my garden, eating all the carrots."

"What?"

"Run along, little girl," the officer said dismissively. "I have a stack of paperwork higher than the Empire State Building, and I got no time for kiddie pranks!"

"But—"

"Shoo!"

.·•·.

Reaching for her cell phone, Anna dialed her father's number with a shaky hand.

Please ring. Please ring. Please listen to me for once. Please listen.

A familiar voice answered, and Anna quickly started shrieking, "Dad! Dad! You have to believe me—" Anna broke off when she realized it was just a recording:

"I am currently overseas and won't be checking my messages regularly. I will return your call when I am back in New York on Wednesday evening. Thank you."

Feeling her heart sink down to the soles of her shoes, Anna trudged home. Never before had she felt so alone. She leaned against the outside of her building and began to sob long, uncontrollable sobs that shook her whole body. Her father was going to die. There was nothing she could do. And the last words she had said to him were *I hate you.*

When she got upstairs, she wiped the tears streaking her face, scrunched up her face, and thought. Really thought. So, the police wouldn't help her. Anna reached for the phone. She knew a few people who would...

CHAPTER 26

The Professionals

"**Anna, what's** the big emergency? I had to leave my sauce simmering right in the middle of *Killer Cucumbers II*!"

Anna smiled grimly at Quenton. "Thanks for making it. This way. Everyone's in here." Anna strode across the lobby to her office and opened the door. Rachel, Todd, Clea and Amy sat scrunched together on the sofa with bewildered expressions on their faces.

"Is everything all right, Anna?" Todd stood up as she entered the room, his blue eyes full of concern.

"Yeah, what's the big emergency?" Rachel asked.

Anna sat down in her desk chair. "I'll tell you guys in a minute. We're just waiting on one other person..."

"Hi, Anna," said a nasal voice from the doorway.

"What's he doing here?" Quenton blurted.

Anna whirled around. "I'm in trouble. Big trouble. And I need a plan. Simon's a game player. He excels in all sorts of games. He was the one who got the flag down and let the West Kingdom into the castle in the Cyber Kingdom war!"

"That was *Simon?*" Quenton said incredulously. "That was like the critical moment in the war. Man, you're like a gaming *legend!*"

Anna looked at the short boy with glasses slouching in her doorway. "I think Simon can help us come up with a plan to catch Donny 'the Meatball' Fratelli."

There was a silence.

And then everyone spoke at once: "Are you nuts?" "We went over this already." "We can't do anything." "We've got no help!"

"It's different now," said Anna quietly. "He's going to kill my father."

There was a loud gasp.

"Donny's one of my patients," Anna explained. "I've been treating him. At first because I didn't know who he was, and then because what goes on in my sessions is supposed to be kept confidential, I wasn't allowed to tell anyone."

Anna began to pace the small room. "Donny doesn't know who I am. But his next hit is on my father. You see, Mr. Who and my father are contenders for a big government shipping contract. Mr. Who wants my father out of the way so he can win it." Anna halted. "The CIA is planning on moving the bioweapon very soon. Mr. Who wants them to use one of his ships to transport it so that he can sneak it off."

Anna felt her eyes begin to sting, and she took a deep

breath to calm herself. "Donny's going to kill my father this Wednesday night."

"Right after Parents' Day," breathed Rachel.

Anna nodded.

"Jeez, Anna. Why are you telling this to us? You should be telling the police!" Quenton cried.

"I did...I tried. They don't believe me."

"They never believe you," Todd said softly, his eyes full of sympathy.

Anna smiled sadly and looked around her office. "So I called you guys. Can you help me?"

Everyone in the room nodded slowly. "Of course, Anna."

Anna turned to Simon. "What do you say? Can you come up with a plan to catch the Meatball and Mr. Who before Wednesday night?"

Simon looked at everyone in the room, who were all looking at him. "I'll do my best." Then he turned to Anna and smiled. "I'm glad you called me."

Three hours later, there was no plan.

Every idea someone had come up with had been shot down as they realized it would not work. In a few more hours, Anna's friends would have to start heading home or risk getting grounded. Anna called for a five-minute break.

"You young folk have sure been working hard in there!" Percy said, looking up from his green notebook as they all stretched their legs in the lobby.

"Yeah, we have—we have—" Anna shook her head, too upset to speak.

"A science project," Rachel cut in, stepping forward.

"And Anna's just afraid we won't finish in time," added Quenton.

"Well, it's not life-or-death, now is it?" Percy said with a grin. "It's just school."

Anna gulped. Todd stepped forward and put his arm around her.

"Percy," Anna said, looking up suddenly. "You wouldn't happen to have any advice on how to catch a criminal in there, would you?"

All the kids were silent as Percy quickly flipped through his green notebook, mumbling to himself. Finally he looked up and shook his head. "Sorry, Miss Anna, I don't."

"Thanks anyway, Percy," Anna said, shuffling back to her office.

"But I do have this saying," Percy called after them. *"If you hold onto the bone, the dog will follow."*

As Anna shut her office door, Simon slowly turned around, his eyes alive. "That's it! That's it!" he exclaimed in his nasal voice. "Why didn't I think of it before?" He glanced around the room, smiling. *"If you hold onto the bone, the dog will follow,"* he repeated. "Donny 'the Meatball' isn't a dog, so he definitely doesn't like bones... but he sure does love cannolis. Chocolate, of course."

CHAPTER 27

Fudging Yourself

The next morning, Anna met her friends in the school foyer before first period started. They leaned against their lockers, bleary-eyed but determined.

"Listen, I know you guys have gotten very little sleep and were up late working on the plan..." Anna broke off, her chest swelling with gratitude. "I just want to say thank you."

"Anna, we would do anything for you!"

Anna smiled and blinked back tears. She cleared her throat. "So, Todd, what have you got?"

Todd stepped forward and handed her a poster. On it was a picture of a very delicious chocolate cannoli, chocolate frosting dripping down onto the lettering below:

WORLD'S BEST CANNOLIS
At Quenton's Café

Located in the Bendox School

Wednesday

October 15, 2:00pm

"This is great, Todd! It looks delicious, like you could grab it right off of the page and take a bite. Can you just put the school address on it too?"

"Sure thing, Anna."

Anna turned to Quenton. "Do you have your new food stand ready to go?"

"Like you even have to ask," said Quenton. "I've been waiting for this moment since kindergarten. Quenton's Café is gonna be a hit!"

"Good. And you're positive you have a recipe for chocolate cannolis? You do know how to make them?"

Quenton puffed up his chest. "Of course I do!"

"Well, make a lot. I don't want to sell out tomorrow before he gets here. And don't make them too fancy. Keep them basic, close to the original recipe. Donny's pretty picky."

Anna turned to Rachel. "What's up, Rach?"

Rachel proudly held a sheet of paper out to Anna. "I totally wrote the most dramatic article possible. He's a giant killer on the loose! It'll definitely catch everyone's eye as they arrive for Parents' Day."

Anna skimmed the article and nodded at the headline. "Good. Remember to hang it smack in the center of *The Riley News* bulletin board. What about you, Clea?"

Clea handed Anna a pile of glossy photographs of Donny's giant purple suede shoes. "I just brought them all in because I didn't know how many you wanted to use."

"Great!" Anna exclaimed, sifting through the shots. "Pick out four or five of the best ones. These should surround Rachel's article on all sides. I really want everyone to get a visual."

Anna finally turned to Amy. "Is it done?" she asked quietly.

Amy nodded. "I scheduled you a session with Donny this afternoon. He'll be at your office at four."

"And what about Mr. Pierce?"

Amy shuffled her feet. "If I get a chance I think I can swipe his cell phone. No one ever notices me anyway. Then we can see if Mr. Pierce has Donny's number and bring the proof to the police."

Anna turned and looked at Simon. "*Thank you.* The plan is brilliant. If everything goes well, it'll all go down tomorrow...on Parents' Day."

Simon reached for a tissue and loudly blew his nose.

The art room was repainted in a bright, happy yellow color, leaving no trace of the crazy writing that had once covered the walls. The class all sat around the large rectangular table and worked with clay. Anna was relieved to be doing something with her hands so her brain could get a rest from all the planning and worrying.

"So my dad is throwing a huge concert on the roof after Parents' Day." Clea rested a leather clad elbow on the table next to Anna.

"Really?"

"Yeah, it's called Rage on the Roof. I just wanted to give you a special invite." Clea slid a black iridescent ticket toward Anna and clomped away.

"Cool!" Anna slipped the ticket into her pocket and looked around excitedly, when Jacob caught her eye. His head was down but he squinted up at her, seething. At that moment, Anna knew that he had gotten into deep trouble with Principal Rollins.

Quickly, she went back to molding her clay. When she glanced back up again, Jacob had vanished. Warily, she scanned the room for him. And then a large piece of soggy wet clay dropped into the front of Anna's smock, soiling her shirt and skidding down into her lap.

"LOOK, EVERYONE! SMUDGE FUDGED HERSELF FOR REAL THIS TIME!" Jacob stood behind her, pinching his nose. "Gosh, Anna, haven't you been potty-trained yet?"

"Eeeew!" Roselyn and a handful of her well-manicured friends squealed.

Anna looked around the room in embarrassment. Everyone had stopped what they were doing; all eyes were on her. She tried to breathe, controlling the anger that was slowly building inside her.

"I know a special potty training school you could go to..." Jacob said thoughtfully, slowly strolling around the table until he was facing Anna. "You could go to the Smudge School for Sludges," he exclaimed, turning to everyone in excitement. "But I hear it smells very bad there!"

There was more sniggering. Anna could feel her cheeks burning, and she was starting to see little red dots.

"Gosh, Anna," Roselyn said, a sweet smile spread

across her cherubic cheeks. "It's sooo unladylike not to be potty trained. Isn't that right, Amy?"

Roselyn looked toward Amy, waiting for her to nod her head in agreement, but Amy merely sat there, her face pale as she looked down at her clay.

"Amy! Isn't that right?" Roselyn asked again, her voice shrill.

Amy looked across the room at Anna and slowly rose from her chair.

"No, Roselyn, I fudged in my pants this morning," she said quietly as she made her way over to Anna and sat down next to her.

Roselyn looked stunned, her lips parted in disbelief.

"Amy! Where do you think you're going? Come back here this instant!"

Amy looked at Roselyn, a calm expression on her face, and said nothing.

"That's it, Amy! You're through! *It's over!*"

"What are you going to do, Roselyn? Not be her friend anymore?" A hush spread across the room as Anna continued.

"Do you really think you were her friend? Do you think friends act like you do? Friends don't threaten. Friends don't boss you around and make you feel unworthy. Friends support you and make you feel like you can accomplish anything."

As the words left Anna's mouth, she knew they were true, and she looked around the room and saw Quenton, Rachel, Todd and Clea nodding their heads in agreement.

"It's not Amy who has no friends, Roselyn, it's you."

Then Anna directed her attention to Jacob, who was standing rather uncomfortably in the center of the room.

"Jacob, you obviously have some severe insecurity issues. You're loud and obnoxious, and you always need attention, especially if it's at someone else's expense. In fact, you're the classic bully—insecure, immature, having to put someone else down in order to look good." Anna shook her head in disapproval. Then she reached out her hand, holding one of her cards.

"Give me a call. Schedule an appointment with Amy. Maybe we can resolve some of those issues so that you can be a fireman or an astronaut or whatever, and you don't have to just be a bully for the rest of your life."

Slowly, Jacob walked forward and took the card from Anna's outstretched hand and took a seat.

"What's going on in here? What's all the commotion?" their substitute teacher cried, sailing into the room.

Quenton looked at Anna. Then he dumped his clay in his lap and exclaimed, "I fudged myself!"

There was a silence, and then another voice cried, "I fudged myself!"

"Me too!" cried Clea.

"Yeah, I also fudged myself," Todd said with a large smile on his face.

"Yeah, I think I need to go to potty-training school!"

Soon the whole class had fudged themselves, and then the bell rang.

CHAPTER 28

Hold onto the Bone and the Dog Will Follow

Anna sat in her office and tried to look as if everything was normal, but things were not normal at all. This was the moment. If things went well in this session with Donny, Anna might be able to save her father's life tomorrow.

A familiar shape filled the doorway.

"Come on in, Donny."

Donny "the Meatball" Fratelli ducked through the doorway and tromped into the room, seating himself onto the sofa with a massive clunk. "Hi, Anna!"

"So how are you today?" Anna asked, crossing her legs.

"Terrific! I enrolled in beauty school. After tomorrow night, it's a whole new career for me!"

We'll see about that, thought Anna. "Donny, I'd like to talk about the career you have right now. Let's talk about your boss."

"Mr. Who?"

"Yes. Who is Mr. Who?"

Donny shrugged. "I don't know. He's Mr. Who."

"But that's not his real name, is it?"

"Who knows?" Suddenly Donny's humongous frame began to shake, and with it the sofa he was sitting on. Anna was about to bolt from the room when she realized that he was laughing. "Get it?" the large man said between shakes. "*Who* knows! Mr. *Who!*"

"Yes." Anna could feel herself growing frustrated. "That was very clever. Now, what does Mr. Who look like?"

Donny shrugged again. "Don't know. I've never seen his face. He always sits behind this screen thingy during meetings."

"So you've never actually seen him?"

"Nope. Don't think anyone's ever seen the guy's face. Don't think anyone from any of the organizations he runs knows what Mr. Who looks like. Maybe the dead guys do, but I can't really ask 'em and expect an answer, ya know what I mean?"

"What crime organizations does Mr. Who run?"

Donny threw Anna a look like she had just asked him the stupidest question. "All of them. He runs 'em all." He leaned forward on the sofa. "Ya see, if you're not with Mr. Who, you're against him. And if you're against Mr. Who...well, then, you won't exist too much longer, if you get my drift."

Anna nodded. "So he runs...everything."

"Yup. Mr. Who runs a ton of organizations. There's the Oshinko mob, the Burg boys, the Rabble crew, the Fanconi famiglia, and the Gorvaschenko cartel...hey, try saying *that* ten times fast! Gorvaschenko, Gorvaschenko, Gorvaschenko..." Donny's voice trailed off.

Anna felt her heart sink; it didn't look like she was going to get anything on Mr. Who. Instead she decided to focus on Donny, and just get done what she had to do.

"Why don't you sit back, Donny, and close your eyes, and I'm going to do what's called a relaxation exercise on you."

The large man leaned back on the sofa. Soon he was snoring loudly. Anna sat there, staring at the clock, counting the minutes, while Donny "the Meatball" napped like a very large, and very lethal, baby on the sofa. When his time was up, she gently tugged his sleeve.

"OK. That was very good, Donny. How do you feel?"

"Gosh, I don't know. I feel relaxed...like a nice person!"

Anna smiled weakly. "Good, that's a good thing to feel. Well, I have to get going, but feel free to relax here for a couple more minutes and see yourself out when you feel ready."

And with that, Anna turned and made her way toward the door, making sure that Todd's poster—with the picture of a chocolate cannoli and the school's address—fell out of her bag as she exited the room.

Anna lay awake in bed going over the plan again in her head. For some reason, she just could not get to sleep. She rolled over, shutting her eyes tightly, but she kept seeing a humongous pair of purple suede shoes swimming in front of her. Finally, Anna turned on her clock radio, hoping some relaxing music would help.

There are still no signs of Donny "the Meatball" Fratelli, though an elderly woman has come forward claiming that the former hitman rescued her Poodle from an oncoming cab. Another woman says Fratelli helped deliver her baby in a stuck elevator. And shoe-store owner Garcia Lopez says that Donny "the Meatball" Fratelli almost went into a rage at his store this morning when he couldn't find a pair of size-sixteen shoes.

"I told him that we just don't carry shoes that big," said Lopez. "Then he looked real angry. I thought he was gonna wack me with that spoon of his, but he just closed his eyes, breathed real deep, and counted to ten. And I could swear he said the word cannoli…"

Anna clicked off the radio and lay back in bed, staring up at the weird patterns her lamp cast on the ceiling. All of the shadows looked strangely like purple suede shoes.

8 Hours Ago

The Way It's Supposed to Be

Anna awoke in the morning with her teeth gritted, her jaw set, and a determination she'd never experienced before. But when she reached the large red doors of Bendox School, a sudden sadness swept over her. She was pretty sure everyone's parents were going to be at Parents' Day today. Everyone's but hers...

Anna tried to shake off the feeling. She was just about to reach for the door handle when there was a loud screech of tires and a black limousine pulled up to the curb with a jolt. The back doors flung open, and Anna heard a familiar voice.

"Are we too late?"

Anna whirled around to see her mother and father standing at the far end of the Bendox sidewalk next to a pile of luggage. She bolted down the walkway like a plane taking off. Then she stopped short, remembering the last time they had seen each other and the awful things she had said.

"I-I thought you guys weren't coming back until tonight?" Anna managed to get out.

"I canceled all of our meetings. We caught an early flight," Anna's father explained.

The whole city seemed to have grown quiet. All Anna could do was stand there as tears welled up in her eyes,

"Sweetheart, we wanted to make it back for Parents' Day," Anna's mother said apologetically.

The limo pulled away from the curb and disappeared down the block, leaving the small family alone. Anna's mother kneeled down and extended her arms. Her eyes were glassy. "Anna, everything's going to be OK."

Immediately, Anna walked over and leaned into her mother's soft lap, smelling her familiar perfume.

Her mother smiled sadly. "I've been so caught up in work, trying to accomplish something important, that I'd forgotten…. Sweetheart, you are my greatest accomplishment."

Anna's father ruffled her hair. "Your mother and I received a handwritten invitation to Parents' Day from someone, and we started thinking about what you said to us after that fight. And you're right. Your mom and I don't spend nearly enough time with you."

Anna's father's face grew grave. "That certainly doesn't excuse what you did."

"I know, and I'm so, so sorry. I'll never do anything like that again. And I don't hate you. I could never…" Anna shook her head in desperation.

"Shhh, we know that, sweetheart." Anna's mother stroked her hair.

"Do you think you can manage to forgive us?" her father asked.

Anna leaped toward her father and hugged him.

"I'm so sorry, pumpkin." Anna's father smiled, reminding her of the man she used to spend Saturdays in the park with. "You're more important than all the business meetings in the world."

As Anna helped her parents roll their luggage into the school foyer, she felt a deep swelling of happiness inside her chest. *This is how life is supposed to be.*

6 Hours Ago

CHAPTER 30

Parents' Day

Anna was about two steps into the foyer when she remembered a minor little detail—that Donny 'The Meatball' Fratelli was supposed to kill her father today. She stopped in her tracks and opened her mouth to warn him, but only half of a word came out, "Da—"

"Anna, honey, what's wrong?" her mother asked, looking back.

Anna tried to keep her cool. The plan was in place. Everyone was doing their part. The plan would work. It had to work. It would work.

"Nothing. Just a fly that flew in my mouth. KHACK!" Anna faked a cough. The best way to protect her mom and dad was to keep them in the dark for now. Then she would know exactly where they were and could steer them out of danger. "Let's go! What are we waiting for?"

The Smudges joined the other families socializing in the main hallway. Everyone's parents were there. The Cohens had arrived in Mr. Cohen's Light Mobile, much to Quenton's embarrassment. Rachel was tugging her mother around by the sleeve, talking a hundred miles an hour. Even Jacob's parents showed, his mother balancing on five-inch stiletto heels, and his father wearing a pair of shiny sunglasses even though they were inside. Anna couldn't tear her eyes away from Mr. Pierce. He kept taking a small phone out of his pocket, walking off to a corner, and suspiciously punching things into it. Anna threw Amy a look and she nodded knowingly and disappeared.

But the biggest hit by far was Clea's dad, Rage Rodriguez, who arrived on a big flame-colored Harley-Davidson with a large iguana resting on his shoulder. He walked the iguana around the hallways on a leash, followed by an entourage of leather-clad bikers.

Everyone except Mr. Pierce stopped to read the Riley News bulletin board. He was too busy looking for his missing cell phone. But the eye-catching article garnered many murmurs from worried parents, and people stopped to stare at the accompanying photos showcased in the middle of the board:

BEWARE THE MAN WITH THE PURPLE SHOES!

At gym class, Ms. McGee was waiting with her whistle. She passed out some spoons and hardboiled eggs, and they all raced, balancing the eggs on their spoons from one side of the gym to the other. Todd and his father won the race,

reaching the other side with an unbroken egg before anyone else.

In the math room, Ms. Musashi wore a purple suede
outfit, greeting everyone with a smile stretched across her
face like a rubber band. Anna immediately complimented
her on her outfit and introduced her parents.

"Very nice to meet you," Ms. Musashi mumbled
uncomfortably. "I'm not used to all these people. You'll
have to excuse me." And she started toward the door, only
to turn back around and say, "Your daughter is wonderful." And then she left the room, and no one saw her for
the rest of the day.

"Well it's nice to know someone else knows just how
special our little girl is," Anna's father said, putting an
arm around her.

Anna smiled as she walked down the hall between her
parents.

"Wow, she sure is a character!" Mr. Cohen exclaimed,
coming up behind Anna and her parents.

"And you're one to talk, Dad," Quenton mumbled.
"Your shirt needs batteries!"

Quenton was in a rather bad mood because his dad had
insisted on wearing a shirt that, when you flipped a little
switch, flashed with different-colored lightbulbs.

"I told him he'd better not wear that thing to the concert tonight."

"Well, if he does, you can just pretend you don't know
him," Anna suggested.

Quenton groaned, "You should have seen the hat he

wanted to wear. It was a sombrero covered with blinking lightbulbs! That's when I drew the line. You know? I told him he wouldn't have a son anymore if he walked out the door in that thing."

Anna tried to suppress a grin.

"I'm telling you, Anna. You have it good."

Anna glanced back at her parents, who were now deep in conversation with the Cohens. She walked over to them as they entered the science room and took her father's hand, squeezing it tight.

CHAPTER 31

Mr. Who?

A little before two o'clock, Anna scampered toward the cafeteria, eager to get a head start, but skidded to a stop when she spotted a familiar figure standing in the hallway, holding a mug of coffee and looking up at all the art and haiku poems hanging for Parents' Day. Anna quietly joined her, remembering the very first time they met and how different she felt now.

"I know you sent that invitation to my parents."

"I'm glad to see that they came," replied Ms. Sinclair.

Anna looked up at the wall and pointed at one of the poems. "You know, I dedicated mine to her." Most kids had dedicated theirs to sisters or brothers or parents, but on Anna's haiku, in neat loopy handwriting, it said: *For Mrs. Summer.*

Ms. Sinclair's eyes grew glassy. "Thank you, Anna. That means a lot."

Anna nervously looked at the big clock. It was almost time.

"Ms. Sinclair, no matter what happens today, no matter how things turn out, I just want you to know that I tried."

Ms. Sinclair's eyes darkened. She looked down at Anna strangely, but before she could say anything, a flood of parents and kids filled the hallway, sweeping Anna up in the rush as they headed into the cafeteria for snacks. Anna had instructed her parents to wait for her in the classroom to keep them safe. She told them it would be too crowded in the cafeteria. And from the look of things, she was right.

Anna glimpsed Quenton wearing a very professional-looking chef's hat and standing proudly behind his new food stand. She quickly wedged herself behind a pillar across the room to watch. She had to keep herself scarce for when Donny showed up. After all, she didn't want him to recognize her.

Anna stood there for a few minutes, intently searching the crowd for her very large patient, when Simon walked right by her. And then something occurred to her. Leaving her hiding place, Anna followed Simon out of the cafeteria. She found him down a secluded corridor finishing up a phone call.

"Simon?"

Simon whirled around. "Oh. Hey, Anna. Listen, I was just calling my doctor—"

"Simon, how did you know Donny 'the Meatball' Fratelli likes chocolate cannolis?"

Simon shrugged his small shoulders. "I don't know. You must have told me."

Anna shook her head. "No, I didn't."

Simon sighed impatiently. "Well, you must have mentioned it or something. Listen, Anna, I think I might have Uveitis. My eyes are hurting pretty bad. So I have to call Dr. Gorvaschenko…"

And then it hit Anna like a really large brick. She heard Donny's voice in her head: "*Mr. Who runs a ton of organizations. There's the Oshinko mob, the Burg boys, the Rabble crew, the Fanconi famiglia and the Gorvaschenko cartel…*"

Stunned, Anna looked at Simon. It all began to fall into place—all the absences, all the supposed doctor's appointments, the strange illnesses to keep everyone away from him. Anna looked at Simon Spektor…really looked…taking in his extra-thick glasses, his neat haircut, his hopelessly sad bowtie, his bad posture. A disguise. It was all a disguise.

"I know who you are," she said quietly.

Simon looked confused. "Um, that's good…good to know. I know who you are too. Listen, Anna, I kind of—"

"I know *who* you are."

Simon stood there, speechless, slouched over his cell phone, looking very confused. And then suddenly he stood up straighter. Simon Spektor seemed to grow a full three inches in size. He rolled his shoulders back and cracked his neck to one side, stretching it out. He took his glasses off, blinked a couple times, and then turned to look at Anna. An expression she had never seen before settled over Simon Spektor's features, making him look like a different person. "How did you know?" said a voice that was no longer nasal but as smooth as silk.

Anna took a step back. "The names. The names of the doctors you're always visiting—they're the same names as the crime organizations you run."

A slow smile spread across Simon's eerie face. "Very good, Anna. You get a gold star."

Anna glared at him.

"But here's the real question: What are you going to do about it?

"I'm going to turn you in."

Simon eyed Anna with cold steel-gray eyes, and for the first time Anna felt scared. Really scared. Then the boy tilted his head back and let loose an odd laugh. "Turn me in? With what? What proof do you have?" He leered at her. "You've got nothing, Smudge. No physical evidence, no eyewitnesses, nothing!"

Anna opened her mouth but closed it again. She felt a large swell of anger. "Mrs. Summer went crazy when she found out Mr. Who was just a kid, just one of her students! What did you say to her? She was your teacher! How could you do that to her?"

But Simon just tilted his head back and laughed. "Maybe I was just sick of finger painting."

Anna clenched her hands. "I don't know how, but I'm going to get you! You've hurt so many people. You almost—you almost had my father killed!"

"Oh, don't take it so personally, Anna." Simon spread

his hands out into a helpless gesture. "After all, it's just a game. One big game. You taught me that."

"No," Anna stuttered, "I didn't mean...I didn't mean—"

"Anna? Anna?"

Anna shut her mouth and slowly turned around. Her heart was beating so fast she thought it would explode.

"There you are, pumpkin!" Anna's father waved from down the hall and began to walk toward them. "Your mother and I have been looking for you. That cannoli stand is selling out fast. Do you want me to get you one?"

Anna stood there, frozen, feeling as though she was trapped in her darkest nightmare. And then, down the hall, she saw Donny 'the Meatball' Fratelli trudge by, the poster Anna had dropped at their last session in his hand. He disappeared into the cafeteria.

"Anna, aren't you going to introduce me to your little friend?" Anna's attention snapped back to her father.

"Hello, I'm Simon Spektor," said a nasal voice.

Mortified, Anna watched Simon stretch his arm out in front of her and take her father's hand, giving it a firm shake.

"So are you one of Anna's classmates, Simon?"

"Yes, sir. Yes, I am. But I'm afraid not for much longer." Simon looked right at Anna. "I'm actually in a foreign exchange program. You knew that, right, Anna? I'll be attending a boarding school overseas."

"How exciting! When will you be leaving?"

"As soon as possible."

Anna clenched her hands, feeling her anger about to

bubble over. How dare he talk to her father! She had to get her father away from him. Anna glanced down the hall, looking for some way out.

"I'd love Anna to see more of the world," Her father commented. "Which boarding school will you be going to?"

"Maester Loch."

"Maester Loch?" Mr. Smudge repeated. "I've never heard of it."

Anna turned to her father. Her whole face was on fire. "Dad, you probably should go—"

And then the screams started—loud, piercing, terrified screams, and the pounding of feet as people began to run from the cafeteria. "AHHH! IT'S HIM! IT'S HIM!"

"What on earth?" Anna's father exclaimed. "Anna, you and your friend better wait here while I go see what's going on."

But Anna already knew what was going on. After all, she was part of the plan. It was all just one big game, and Simon had used her and her friends as pawns. But Anna wasn't going to stand for it. As her father hurried off down the hallway, Anna turned back to Simon. But he was gone.

Frustrated, Anna smacked a locker. On the front, in small silver letters, it said "MasterLock." *Lies!* she thought. *It's all been a bunch of lies! This can't be happening! He can't just get away. He can't just disappear without a trace!*

More screams sounded from the cafeteria, followed by the clang of pots and pans, and then Anna knew what she had to do. She had to try to catch Mr. Who before he left the country. And she knew just the person who could help her...

Anna wove her way through fleeing people to the cafeteria. Parents and kids were running in every direction, screaming and shouting. It was total chaos.

"Anna!"

Quenton was wedged into a corner, his chef's hat hanging off the side of his head.

"Anna, Donny 'the Meatball' Fratelli's here! He's here! The plan worked!"

"Where is he?"

"In there! In the cafeteria! By my booth!"

"Listen, Quenton." Anna leaned forward and grabbed Quenton by the shoulders. "The plan has changed. I need Donny."

"You what?"

"I need Donny to help me catch Mr. Who."

Quenton's jaw dropped. "It's Mr. Pierce?"

"No."

"Then *who* is he?"

Anna sighed. "You wouldn't believe me if I told you. Now listen, there's no time. I need you and the others to create some sort of distraction out front so the cops don't come back here right away. OK?"

Quenton nodded and then ran down the empty hallway toward the front of the school. Anna burst through the cafeteria door, jumping and diving over overturned chairs and tables until she saw him. He was pretty hard to miss—

a massive figure stuffing the last of the chocolate cannolis into his pockets. Police sirens sounded outside, and Anna could hear voices calling out orders over a loudspeaker.

"Donny!"

The large man whirled around. "Anna!" he said with a large smile.

Anna rushed forward and grabbed the large man by the arm, dragging him toward the cafeteria kitchen. "We've got to get out of here!"

"But I gotta tell ya something."

"Donny, not now...come on!" But Anna stopped tugging, realizing that it was like trying to move a very large tree that didn't want to be moved.

"Anna," Donny looked down at her, "Your pop's in trouble."

Anna opened her mouth and then closed it again. "You know who I am?" she asked.

"Yeah, I found out when Mr. Who called telling me to come here and do the hit early. He said he knew exactly where Mr. Smudge would be."

Anna's breath caught in her throat; she looked toward the cafeteria doors. "Did you do it?"

"No." Donny's jaw tightened. "I didn't, and I won't! I would never kill your pop, Anna... unless, of course, you wanted me to?"

Anna vigorously shook her head no.

"You're my shrink," Donny said, his eyes crinkling up at the corners. "You helped me like no one in my whole life. I owe you. You got me on the straight and arrow."

"Narrow," Anna corrected.

"What?"

"The expression. It's 'straight and narrow.'"

"Oh."

Suddenly it hit Anna with full force that her father was safe. She felt herself begin to tear up with relief, but then she remembered Simon. "Come on, Donny!" she cried, tugging on the large man's arm again. "Come on! We had to be out of here, like, five minutes ago."

Anna dragged her large patient through the cafeteria kitchen and to the emergency exit in the rear. "Follow me!" Anna ran toward the heavy door and kicked it open. Immediately a loud alarm began clanging. Covering her ears from the deafening sound, Anna stepped out into a deserted alleyway and looked around. How in the world were they going to get out of here without being seen?

And then a dark car with dark windows screeched to a halt. A window rolled down. "Get in," said Ms. Musashi.

3 Hours Ago

The Glass Room

Anna and Donny "the Meatball" Fratelli sat in the backseat of the dark car next to Ms. Musashi, who was dressed all in black. Her infamous stick had a black tip. A mysterious man, also dressed in black, sat in the driver's seat. Puzzled, Anna turned to her math teacher.

"What-what's going on?"

"I was just in the neighborhood," Ms. Musashi said smoothly. "I saw you and your friend here and thought you could use a lift."

"Hey, that was real nice!" Donny said, busy eating one of the chocolate cannolis he had stuffed into his pocket.

"So where are you going?" Ms. Musashi asked.

Anna shook her head. "But I don't understand. What are you—"

"Questions simply cannot and will not be answered!" Ms. Musashi snapped. "There's no time!"

"Hey!" Donny growled, putting his cannoli down. "Don't talk to my shrink like that!"

"Donny, it's OK." Anna rested a hand on his large arm.

"So...where are we going, Smudge?"

Anna sighed and looked back up at Donny. "Listen, Donny, I need you to help me find Mr. Who."

"I told you, Anna, I don't know who he is."

"I do." Anna raised her chin up. "I know exactly who he is. All I need to know is where to find him. You said you went to a bunch of meetings, Donny. Where? Where were those meetings?"

Donny shifted uncertainly in his seat. "Well, I don't know if I should—"

"Donny, you told me you wanted to start a new life, right? Start it on the right foot. Do it right this time around!"

The large man was silent. Then he looked up and barked, "Driver, take us to the Holland Tunnel."

.◉.

"Are you sure it's here?"

Anna, Donny "the Meatball" Fratelli and Ms. Musashi kept close to the inside wall of the Holland Tunnel as traffic whizzed by them.

"Yup," Donny said, examining the tiles on the wall. "It should be right about—"

"Here!" Ms. Musashi pointed to a small etching with her stick. It was of a hawk, a cheetah and a crocodile.

"Yup, that's it."

"But what does it stand for?" Anna asked as Donny began knocking on the tile in a weird rhythm.

"Don't know."

"It's everything he dominates," Ms. Musashi replied quietly. "The hawk represents air, the cheetah is an animal of the land, and the crocodile resides in the water. His many organizations all over the world build airplanes, buildings, and ships. Basically, he controls air, land, and sea."

The etching began to spin, slowly at first and then faster. The large man told them to lean against the wall. There was a hissing noise, like a pressure seal opening, and they fell through to the other side.

.●.

Anna gulped and looked around the glass room. "I don't like it here."

"Me neither," Donny said, stepping onto the glass floor as lightly as possible.

"We need to look around for clues," said Ms. Musashi, striding into the room and ignoring the dark water surrounding them on all sides. She began to pat down the glass table and search beneath the glass chairs.

Anna held her breath and took a step. It seemed like she was walking on nothing. Then she spotted something. It was a slip of paper resting on the floor.

"I found something!" Anna cried, bending down. She picked up the note and began to read it aloud.

To whom it may concern,

Do you honestly think I'm so stupid as to return to a glass room? After all, glass can break.

Sincerely,

Mr. Who

Anna looked up at Ms. Musashi and Donny, her eyes wide with terror. Ms. Musashi yanked the note from Anna's hand and studied it closely.

"This is fresh ink."

"Are you sure?"

"I've graded enough papers in my time to know when homework was done at the last minute," Ms. Musashi said. Then she looked around thoughtfully. "He wasn't in the Holland Tunnel—we would have seen him. There must be another way out of here that he used."

She handed the note back to Anna and began to circle the room. When Anna looked back down at the note, a drop of something splashed onto it. Then there was another drop. And another.

"Omigod, there's a leak!"

Donny quickly dove toward the door connecting back to the tunnel, pounding the same rhythm that he did to get them in. Then he waited. Then he did it again, and waited.

"The door doesn't work," Ms. Musashi said. "The little bugger had the thing reprogrammed."

Water was beginning to seep through the ceiling now. Anna watched it trickle in, trying to hold back tears.

"I DON'T WANNA DIE!" Donny cried.

"Just keep quiet and be still!" Ms. Musashi scolded. "I've found something."

Ms. Musashi was behind the dark partition at the head of the glass table. Anna quickly walked over to find her math teacher squatting on the glass floor. She had pushed aside the chair behind the partition to reveal a trap door and a control panel with lights. She looked up at Anna and Donny.

"I just have to call the carrier tube back from the other end of the chute and then open this trap door."

Anna looked behind her at the crack in the glass ceiling. It was much bigger now and was slowly branching off into other cracks that spread down the wall like a spider web.

"Darn it!" Ms. Musashi pushed a large button on the control panel again and again. The room began to make an eerie creaking noise, like a door that needed oiling. The cracks in the glass spread faster; water was pouring in steadily now.

"What are you doing?" Anna moaned. She could feel tears streaking down her cheeks and onto her neck, but she didn't care. "WHAT'S GOING ON?"

"I told you already," Ms. Musashi answered.

"BUT I DON'T UNDERSTAND!" Anna cried. She was so terrified she was shaking uncontrollably...and still the water seeped in, cold and dark.

"Miss Smudge!" Ms. Musashi snapped, holding down the large button on the control panel, sweat pouring from her forehead. "I understand you recently had a field trip to the New York Public Library?"

Anna looked at her math teacher in disbelief. Behind her, Donny began to howl in fear as water covered the floor of the room, swooshing into their shoes.

"SO?" Anna shrieked. "SO WHAT?!"

"So, if you had been paying attention, as Mr. Spektor was, you would have learned about the pneumatic tube system that was used to send call slips down to the underground book shelves. This is just like that, only bigger."

The water was up to their ankles now, and rushing in rapidly. The hard glass was creaking so loudly under the pressure of the water, Anna covered her ears with both hands to block out the horrible sound. She looked around frantically. The room wouldn't hold for much longer. And all around them was black...just black...the dark river of the Hudson surrounding them on all sides...and it flowed into the glass room faster and faster.

"I DON'T WANNA DIE!" Donny wailed.

This time Ms. Musashi didn't tell him to be quiet.

Anna let loose a sob and shook her head in disbelief. This had been one of the best days of her life, surrounded by her parents and her friends, and now she'd never see them again. She let loose another sob. And it was all because of Simon! Simon Spektor! He had led them here! He had planned it all! Like one of his stupid games!

Suddenly there was a loud sucking sound and then a clank.

"The carrier tube is here," Ms. Musashi said in her thin voice, but Anna could sense she was relieved. "I just have to get this chair out of the way...and open this trap door so we can get in..." Ms. Musashi tried to push Mr. Who's chair out of the way, but it was stuck.

"DARN IT!" she screamed, finally losing her cool.

"Here, let me try." Donny kicked the chair off its hatch and yanked the trap door open. Behind it, a small bobsled-looking vehicle sat in the chute.

"Oh, I get it," Donny said with a smile. "It's like sucking the middle out of a cannoli!"

"You two first," Ms. Musashi said, a determined look on her face.

"No way!" Anna cried. "We all go together!"

"MISS SMUDGE," Ms. Musashi was screaming to be heard over the rushing water and the loud creaking. "YOU ARE STILL TALKING TO YOUR TEACHER AND WILL FOLLOW INSTRUCTIONS!"

Anna stubbornly stared at Ms. Musashi, tears streaming down her face. She shook her head.

"Anna," Ms. Musashi gently took Anna's chin in her hand. "The carrier will not move with all of our combined weight. Math is a system of absolute rules, remember?"

Anna nodded.

"Besides, Mr. Fratelli has to survive. He is the only link to Mr. Who's identity, and he has the best chance of stopping him when you exit the tunnel."

Ms. Musashi turned to Donny and threw him a look. The large man nodded. He turned to Anna, who was openly sobbing now. Her tears flowed as freely as the river water pouring into the room. "Come on, Anna." The large man climbed into the carrier.

"GO!" Ms. Musashi snapped.

Anna climbed into the carrier, shaking with fear, shaking with grief; she was shaking so hard, her whole body hurt.

"Don't worry about me, Smudge." A tinge of fear flickered across Ms. Musashi's face, but then it was gone. "This stick isn't just a color-coordinated fashion accessory."

The last thing Anna saw was Ms. Musashi's awkward smile as she slammed the carrier door shut, and then there was just blackness and a loud whooshing sound as the carrier was sucked down the chute. In the far distance, Anna could hear the sound of glass shattering and the roar of water crashing in...and then there was nothing.

Anna popped the lid of the chute open. The surrounding floor was littered with broken easels, pastels and paint tubes, and as she pushed a ripped canvas out of the way, it suddenly dawned on her where they had surfaced.

"Where are we?" asked Donny.

"Mrs. Summer's—" But Anna didn't finish. She had turned to look at the other side of the room...but it wasn't there. Instead, a crumbled mountain of bricks and bedrock littered the area—the wall had been blown apart! Anna gasped in horror as she looked right into the next building. The old Bendox gymnasium was strewn with rubble and great heaps of cement. Bodies lay lifeless in the wreckage, dazed men in army fatigues stumbled around, holding very bad wounds.

"Looks like he used that little bomb," muttered Donny. "But it doesn't seem like it was as itty-bitty as he thought." The large man pointed toward a path of blood extending out from underneath the bleachers, weaving its way up the great mound of rubble and continuing into Mrs. Summer's building, where it abruptly stopped in front of a door. Anna quickly yanked the door open. "It's a stairwell!"

A loud whipping noise could be heard from above them.

"He's got the bioweapon!" she shouted, racing up to the roof. There was more blood on the stairs, large puddles of it. Donny was right—Mr. Who must have gotten hurt.

Anna rammed the door open with her shoulder and dashed out onto the rooftop, where the noise was deafening and a rough wind nearly blew her back down the stairs. A helicopter was hovering, Dr. LeGrande's large sealed box dangling from its bottom. And then the helicopter began to rise up into the sky.

"NO!" Anna shouted, running after it, her fists in the air. "NO!"

The helicopter climbed higher, its blades whirling faster and faster. Anna glimpsed a severe looking woman in a pinstriped suit seated in the driver's seat and a short figure hunched over in the back. And then the helicopter was just a large pinprick in the sky. He was gone.

Anna had a sinking feeling in her chest. She looked down at her feet and saw a pile of crimson-stained tissues and an empty tissue box. And then something white fluttered down from the sky and landed on the tarmac in front of her shoe. It was a note written in garish red, messy letters:

Blood has been shed.
Prepare for war.

CHAPTER 33

The Chief's Office

"...and that's everything."

Anna's voice felt raw from talking nonstop for so long. She looked around for some water, but there was only a large mug of coffee. She picked it up with both hands and took a sip before spitting it out into the Chief's garbage. "Yuck!"

"I can't believe it. All along, Mr. Who was just a kid?"

Anna nodded.

The Chief slammed his fist onto the desk, frustrated. "And here I was all this time, looking at parents and teachers and doggone grown-ups!"

There was a knock, and an officer stuck his head in the door. Anna recognized him immediately. He was the cop who had told her to "shoo" that day she had run to the precinct. He glanced at her nervously and cleared his throat. "Um, sir, we got the test results back for this." he held out a plastic bag with an empty tissue box in it.

"And?" barked the Chief impatiently. "And, you imbecile?"

"And there were no fingerprints on it other than the girl's."

The Chief picked up his mug and hurled it across the room. The officer quickly shut the door just as the mug hit it and shattered into pieces. "Gone!" the Chief yelled. "The greatest criminal mastermind of our time—gone without a freakin' trace! And once again, we got nothing! We don't even know exactly what it is that he escaped with."

"I told you," Anna said quietly. "It was a biological weapon."

The Chief eyed Anna. "You know, when we arrived at the scene, all the bodies were gone. Sure, there was tons of blood, but no bodies." The Chief leaned forward in his chair. "The CIA are denying that they were ever holding anything in that old school gymnasium."

Anna shook her head. "They were," she insisted. "That's the whole reason why Mr. Who wanted Mrs. Summer's art studio. Because it's right next door. The two buildings share a wall, for goodness sake!" Anna sighed. "Don't you see, I messed up his plan. He wanted the CIA to use one of *his* ships to transport the weapon so that he could steal it out from under their noses quietly. But when I found out who he was, it threw his whole schedule off. So he had resort to his backup plan—blowing out the brick wall connecting the two buildings. And things got messy. And he got hurt. And now he's pissed."

"Look, I believe you, Anna. But this kid's as slippery as soap. And the CIA are covering up the whole fiasco. They're saying that nothing happened. They're tellin' me that old school gym is just under construction, that's all. And they didn't know anything about that teacher of yours." The Chief sighed, and a glimmer of fear shone in his tired eyes. "All I know is, whatever Mr. Who took...it must be something unimaginable."

Anna nodded gravely, remembering the sealed plastic room and the scared looks on the faces of the men in the hazmat suits.

"Listen, Miss Smudge," the Chief awkwardly cleared his throat, "I just want to apologize that no one would listen to you before, when you came in about your father."

"It's OK. He's safe now."

"Yeah, well, if one of these muck-mucks had listened, we probably could've made the arrest of a decade."

"We'll just have to keep looking." Anna clenched her hands and rose from her chair. "We'll catch him, Chief," she said, her voice filled with venom. "Even if it's not until my sixteenth birthday, I promise you that I won't stop until Simon Spektor is eating stale bread in a jail cell!"

"I'm sure you won't, Miss Smudge." The Chief raised his eyebrows. "By the way, it was pretty impressive, getting Donny to turn himself in the way you did. How'd ya swing that?"

Anna shrugged and walked to the door.

"Hey, what's your hurry?"

Anna exited the Chief of Police's office, calling out

behind her, "I have a show to catch. Haven't you heard? It's all the rage."

.•.

Dozens of stagehands scurried around, setting up massive strobe lights and equipment on the Bendox rooftop for the big Rage Rodriguez concert. Anna and her friends sat in a roped-off VIP section, their table piled high with soda and mini desserts.

"I am psyched!" exclaimed Anna. "I've never heard Rage Rodriguez live before."

"Yeah, dad's pretty good," said Clea. "You should hear him in the shower."

An electronic buzzing sounded and Clea snapped open Mr. Pierce's cell phone. "WHAT?!" she barked into the phone. "I thought I told you never to call me again! I don't care if you make me a billion dollars a year. We're done!" Clea shut the phone with a victorious smile. "Ah, revenge is sweet."

"Yeah, but not as sweet as these desserts," chimed Quenton, lifting a hazelnut brownie to his lips. "I used real giandua chocolate, you know."

"Those cannolis were delicious today, Quenton," said Todd. "Maybe you should think about opening your own place?"

"Yeah..." Quenton gazed off dreamily.

"We should have a toast," suggested Amy.

"To Anna Smudge!" exclaimed Todd.

Everyone clinked their glasses together. "Yes. To Anna!"

Anna blushed, looking down at the table. "And to Ms. Musashi," she added softly.

There was a heavy silence and then everyone scooted back their chairs and rose to their feet. They raised their glasses high into the air for a long moment to remember their fallen math teacher.

Anna wiped away a tear and surveyed the glittering Manhattan cityscape spread out before them. "I still can't believe he got away. He could be anywhere right now."

"And now he's got that—that box with him," added Amy.

"Let's face it, guys," said Rachel. "We still have no idea *what* exactly is in that box."

"But it's up to us to get it back," proclaimed Todd.

"And we will," said Anna. "We owe it to Ms. Musashi."

Suddenly a large gust of wind swept a business card through the air like a small white butterfly. It landed in Rachel's soda, and she plucked it out before peering at Anna curiously. "What I'd like to know is how Anna got Donny to turn himself in."

Everyone turned to look at Anna, waiting for her reply.

Anna Smudge smiled mysteriously. "A good shrink never tells."

Then the strobe lights flashed like lightning, the drums exploded like thunder, and Rage Rodriguez screamed his very first note.

Acknowledgments

Steps up to podium. Taps microphone to make sure it is on.

This book has been a long time in the making. And honestly, I don't think it would have been possible without the help of some very special people. I'd like to thank...

Rena Pacella for the late-night advice and stellar editing. Rina Bander for minding my P's and Q's. Sara Parks, Lee Waxenberg, and Doug McEachern for all of their incredibly insightful feedback. Jeff Capshew for his wonderful friendship and generosity.

Greg Collins for breaking all of the rules and caring about this book as much as I do. Glenn Fabry for bringing to life all of the characters that have lived inside my head for six years. Greg Horn for summing up an entire book in one stunning image. Todd Masters for getting the art to pop off of the page.

Geoff Roesch and his brilliant cohorts Eric McCarthy and Danny Ramos at Volcano. Scott Strong for his amazing animation. Mark Malkoff and Michael Kaminer for their immense support and enthusiasm. Alison Hill, Marisa Aguilar, Susan Champlin, and Jim DeNuccio at Current PR—the best cheerleading team a girl could ask for!

Norm Hood and Leta Davis for proving any of this was even possible. Rebecca Sherman who believed in Anna at the very beginning. And Gregory Rutty who believed in Anna at the very end.

My parents, Franci and Paul; Clyde, Sandra, and the rest of my Texas family; and my Canadian family—Franca, Mario, Jesse, and Julianna Alibrando. I love you guys more than chocolate cannolis!

Steps down from podium. Goes back into darkened cave to write next book.